Airs of Providence

Johns Hopkins: Poetry and Fiction
John T. Irwin, General Editor

Guy Davenport, *Da Vinci's Bicycle: Ten Stories*
John Hollander, *"Blue Wine" and Other Poems*
Robert Pack, *Waking to My Name: New and Selected Poems*
Stephen Dixon, *Fourteen Stories*
Philip Dacey, *The Boy under the Bed*
Jack Matthews, *Dubious Persuasions: Short Stories*
Guy Davenport, *Tatlin!*
Wyatt Prunty, *The Times Between*
Barry Spacks, *Spacks Street: New and Selected Poems*
Joe Ashby Porter, *The Kentucky Stories*
Gibbons Ruark, *Keeping Company*
Stephen Dixon, *Time to Go*
Jack Matthews, *Crazy Women: Short Stories*
David St. John, *Hush*
Jean McGarry, *Airs of Providence*

AIRS OF PROVIDENCE

JEAN McGARRY

The Johns Hopkins University Press   Baltimore and London

"Providence, 1934: The House at the Beach" originally appeared in *Nantucket Review*.

This book has been brought to publication with the generous assistance of the G. Harry Pouder Fund and the Albert Dowling Trust.

The Johns Hopkins University Press, 701 West 40th Street, Baltimore, Maryland 21211
The Johns Hopkins Press Ltd, London

The paper in this book is acid-free and meets the guidelines for permanence and durability of the Committee on Production Guidelines for Book Longevity of the Council on Library Resources.

Library of Congress Cataloging in Publication Data
McGarry, Jean.
    Airs of providence.
Traced (Johns Hopkins, poetry and fiction)
    I. Title. II. Series.
PS3563.C3636A75 1985   813'.54   85-9805
ISBN 0-8018-2909-7 (alk. paper)

for Robert Gregory

Contents

Airs of Providence

Providence, 1954: Watch

Mrs. Humphries lived in a gray house, two floors, backyard and detached garage, and around her neck hung the aurora borealis Mr. Humphries had given her twenty years after they bought the house, and four months before he died. He knew it, too. His lips were razor thin and the arms he raised out of the bedclothes just bone with a flap of hairy skin. He raised these arms to encompass in a tense and trembling hug, Frances Humphries; the beads hung down on his face and he was glad they did, glad to see she would wear them day in and day out and while he was dying. Lovebirds, he'd say.

Mr. Humphries began to smell sweet like a rose, the nurse said, a few days before it hit him. It hit him at 4:30 in the afternoon, Halloween 1954, when it was raining and dark and the kids were crying up and down the street when their streaming paper bags split and into the rivulet that was the street dropped loose and packaged candy and popcorn, the apples would drop with a thud and the streets, someone said the next day, were paved with sweets. They weren't as thickly paved at 4:00. He was lying then on his left side and Frances, hovering somewhere. She was making a place for herself in his room and this involved a transfer of the day's objects. For today, that Halloween day, there was a tray with a ball of thin white yarn, steel crochet needle, half a white bootie for sister Jane's daughter's infant, Ada, a cup of cocoa and a deck of cards in case he wanted to play a hand, and had the oomph to do it, her prayerbook with an elastic around it to keep in the cards and memories and a black rosary in a thin pile on the yellow painted tray with appliqués, wedding present from someone on his side. Now that she was in the room, and settled in the comfortable chair with the tray across the arms, she heard something from the bed, removed the tray, set it on the floor, and went to see what he was up to.

Henry? He was asleep. His eyes were closed. His arms were bundled together, and the small blanketed column lifted and fell with breath you couldn't hear. The nurse had gone home for the day, a Saturday, after tidying him and arranging his medications on the bureau with an instruction under each bottle. He was having a beautiful death, the nurse told people in the neighborhood she knew knew him, or knew of him. He'd go, she was sure, in his sleep, and peaceful. And that Frances Humphries, she added, is a soldier. She's there every minute with not a complaint on her lips and keeps herself busy, too, and cheerful. The sick don't want another long face around them, she knew that much from nursing the sick and hearing them, or those around them, say it, because it was hard enough, and that was what the wake was for, time enough to let the hard feelings out, although it very rarely happened. By then, most saw the event as a mercy and were glad to see the mortal relieved and at rest. Life goes on, they'd say in a loud whisper right next to the casket. He was a good man, he doesn't look his age, he lived a good life, he suffered a lot at the end, and in the end, God took him. He's better off where he is. Then they'd go sit down on a metal chair placed in rows before the casket with its flowers and candles, and see who was there to pass the time of day, to inquire into the whereabouts of the deceased's immediate and less immediate family, especially the children. New facts would be considered against the impressions and predictions that had been made when, say, little Peggy Curran, now a big girl, was sent to the sisters for grammar school (like all the others), but expelled in fifth grade for swearing so a nun could hear. She had either made good or was still on that track the expulsion had set her on. This was the time to do it, and was what you *could* do to gauge the grief of the widow, because the death was added to everything else, although there were times when it took away something, and the burden was lighter. This was frequently the case and voices were known to drop: the dead were better dead, more alive dead, better regarded and better for everyone else on earth. It hurt no one to say this. This is what had to be said.

The wake was the culmination of the life and of the family's life, and it could be perfect. Mrs. Humphries, settling back on the chair but without the tray, letting her eyeglasses just hang on the smooth black cord, remembered a time—it was a sudden death, heart attack—when the husband, who had had a few before the first night and after the first afternoon, had spoiled it. An out-of-towner had come by, a man with kids in the grammar school twenty years ago, pals with the Lennon children. There were tears on Mr. Lennon's face. Mrs. Humphries remembered that; also his face was red and he reeked; or, at least, if you got up close, you could get a whiff of it, and it wasn't beer. Mr. Jenkins, right in front of Mrs. Humphries in the line filing past the casket, was pumping Jack Lennon's hand, big hands he had, worked construction before the fall and then disabled, when in a loud voice, after a question Mrs. Humphries couldn't quite hear, said: I was sitting, see, on the beach blanket and there she was standing knee-deep in the water—the water was warm that day, 68–70, warm—and she's waving, waving her head off. I felt like saying: turn around, Louise, the water's the other way. All I remember is her waving, bye-bye, then all of a sudden she was gone.

And Jack Lennon, a decent man, not a hard case, laughing so to choke, and Mr. Jenkins, too, though less so. What was so funny? All I remember is the water up to her knees waving bye-bye like a baby. He got control of himself and thank God the crowd hadn't come yet, but Mrs. Humphries felt scandalized; the sound of it would come back to her over the years when she would imagine wakes to come and compare them to wakes of the past. Mr. Humphries laughed when he heard the story, but he wasn't strict: he wasn't lax either, Mass and communion every Sunday and an usher for eighteen years, but he liked his liquor, and when Joe Keefe had his own place on Huron Street—College Tap, Everybody's Campus—Big Harry Humphries, they still called him that from his year at Providence College, starting center forward for the Friars, was in there every afternoon after work for a cold one. He said one; she knew better, but he didn't come home, God rest his soul—she caught herself and flushed at the idea that she was hurrying him—stinking. He could be light, plus he wasn't right there to hear it and have to look down at poor Mrs. lying there, made mock of the one time she could be pretty sure she wouldn't be. Imagine, Mrs. Humphries had said, taking that away from the poor woman, when what else did she have left?

———

Mr. Humphries knew, but he had not accepted it. He was awake and heard her come in, clatter in with that tray full of junk, sit down, get up, snoop around and now she was quiet; he opened his eyes and could see down to the street. He had seen one kid, a small boy wrapped in a wet sheet with red boots sticking out, and a ribbon around his neck to hold the sheet, stumble and lie there in a puddle. It was only when he struggled to his feet that the shopping bag gave way at the bottom and a little pile of candy fell to the sidewalk, things rolling down the street, all those folded napkins unfolding or matting together. Mr. Humphries lifted himself slightly to see. The child looked at the bottom of the bag and felt the wet ragged edges, then he set the bag by the handles down on the sidewalk. He looked around but no one was coming to help; no one was coming to try and steal the candy, was what Mr. Humphries was thinking and smiling as he thought it. The child, with nothing to hold, was looking down at the pile. He ran after the apple—was it an apple or a ball of pop-corn?—recovered it by the leg of the mailbox, replaced it on the pile and covered the whole with the open end of the sack. Mr. Humphries was forced to close his eyes; there she was inquiring. When he opened them again, the boy was gone, just the little ghost left on the sidewalk. Some kids came by, looked, and walked around it. More kids. A boy in a skeleton costume with a pillowcase as a sack walked past, then turned around, yelled at his friends to wait, and gave the sack a kick just to see. He heard their doorbell ring and that was her getting up. The sack ripped again and was starting to blow down the street, but the skeleton caught it, looked at the bottom—Wait up, I said—and put the folded up, broken bag in his own bag, then took it out, and threw it over the pile of candy. It blew away five feet, leave it be. Mr. Humphries lay back. He heard the rocker squeak, then the sound he knew was Mrs. Humphries preparing, then stifling a sigh. He'd hear the inhalation, then a sniff or cough. Once she had started choking and the nurse, who was playing solitaire in her corner, pounded her on the back. The nurse was using a student desk with attached chair, and some of her belongings were in it, some were in the carpet bag she carried with her every day and lay against a leg of the desk. She liked to play cards, do crosswords, read horoscopes and books about birds and flowers. She had a patch of embroidery for a pillowcase she was making for an out-of-town cousin's daughter, but she didn't like to sew in a sickroom. She hadn't said this, but Frances gathered it since that was the first thing she pulled out whenever the women took their tea in the kitchen to get a breather. They both were tea drinkers and used two bags per cup, let the tea get very black, then stirred in the cream and sugar. Filled cookies in an assorted package, or sometimes just bread, butter and sugar kept them alert and satisfied in the middle of a long afternoon. The nurse had never married, so she wasn't the most understanding person in the world, but she didn't hate men, like the rest of them did, and she and Mister could get into a line of talk, very critical—and Frances, who didn't like to hear people knocked, was not among the party—of some of the people in the neighborhood and they'd both be roaring, Mr. Humphries choking like you'd think he was choking to death. They had their moments, too, three people under one roof, and a convalescent—that's what Frances and the nurse called him between themselves, but they knew he wasn't getting better.

———————

The pain, she had said to the lady next door, just out of the hospital with a new baby and hanging a load of diapers out on the line, was terrible. It keeps him up most of the night and what can you do all night long, what is there to think about? He hardly says a word, but I can see it, and once he told me that sometimes it's so bad, he's thought of (Frances didn't know exactly how to put this so she could get the effect of it but without giving scandal) taking his own life. This put a scare into Frances the day he mentioned it, late summer some time—he had been bedridden since spring, and in decline since midsummer, although they had made that one day trip to Ocean Drive when the America's Cup boats were docked. He had always loved the water and loved boats and was proud their own state was the home of this important boat race, something the whole world knew about and paid attention to.

They walked that day; he was able to get out of the car and walk a few feet. She pointed out the flowering wild roses growing so close, as he could see, to the cultivated ones the rich people grew, there in their houses—or not there. Sometimes you couldn't tell: the houses were so big and you couldn't expect them to be right there by the window just as you were looking. At any rate, she said again, speaking to the side of his head because he kept his eyes on the water and on the one boat still out there, its sail pink and flat in the afternoon light, cloudy and humid. But, he said, you could see people on the *boat:* see them? I can see them. She looked, but it was so far away and she didn't know who it was that was on these boats and in these races—he did, he kept up; he knew one country's boat from another, he knew some of the names; he knew the ins and outs of the race and the awful hardships and miseries these men were facing; he had thought about it, and was thinking about it; she didn't interrupt. She let him talk, but he didn't talk for long. He tried to imagine, he told her, what they were doing now, in the slack times, before the race began: polishing brass and wood, he thought, checking instruments, studying maps and currents, tides and what was underneath that smooth surface of ocean on this dull, flat day.

It was a good day. It was his last full day, and he was in pain even that day; she could see it in the way he kept his face turned away and didn't answer sometimes, even a direct question. He never did that. Some husbands weren't that polite to their wives and gave them sharp words, or worse, when they would ask a simple question; some never talked to their wives at all. He did. He explained things she didn't understand and admitted when he didn't understand them either. So, his not answering and also the way she couldn't catch his eye, when normally on an outing like this, he'd meet her eye and hold it, so many times had they seen the same things or heard the same story, gone over the same bump on Rte. 2, or stopped for an ice cream or a drink and a few laughs along the scenic route, or heard other people laugh—the kind of laugh you recognize. She knew he was sick, and—at first she didn't accept it—anxious to die, but now he wasn't so anxious.

That morning, last day of October, it was fresh and clear, no sign of rain; she came into his room and opened the window. She herself was in a fresh blouse, white with a pink stripe, and a plaid skirt; the clear

6

beads around her neck didn't look right with the clothes. She bent over his bed to give him a kiss; she didn't always do this, and he didn't really care one way or the other, but she did, that morning, and first he got the kiss and then the beads sliding over his face. Lovebirds, he said, and held the thought and the feel of the sharp-edged, cool beads. At 4:20, the fog was thick and a car stopped in front of the house. A young woman jumped out of a black Plymouth, from the driver's side; she had a raincoat on over a housecoat and loafers on her feet; the woman scooped up what there was to be scooped up— whatever could it be? she wondered, leaning into the window—from the sidewalk, and into a brown sack she shook open. It was candy, he said. What?

A minute later and it was over. She looked at the bed, a single bed—youth bed, they used to call them; she was sleeping alone in the bed her mother had given them twenty-five years ago. She didn't feel that old. He wasn't old. He shouldn't be in that bed, and so shrunken he was. His eyes were closed now; he was sleeping; his arms bundled close. There was no room in there for her, but more than she expected, or would ever say or think about again, she wanted to climb in there with him. That was the doorbell, but in an hour or so when it would be so dark you didn't know who or what you were getting, she was just going to sit and let it ring.

Penmanship

The blinds were closed, no light escaping, but they were in there. The two kids, April and Margery, Margery the oldest but April still the biggest. April had the two pairs of glasses: the old pair and the new pair. The old pair had fallen into the toilet bowl. Looking out the bathroom window, April saw her friend Sandy make footprints in the no-footprint snow.

Margery was in her own room listening to records. She could either be listening to their parents' old records, now that they didn't listen to records anymore: Mitch Miller, Patti Page, gypsy violin, Frank Sinatra; or 45s. Margery was almost a teenager and April knew what that meant, but Margery didn't think she did because she kept the record player so low April couldn't hear, plus the door locked.

Margery was going through a stage, that's what their mother told Mrs. McKenna when they were food shopping. April acted busy: she arranged the items in her mother's cart, but they didn't say anymore. Big ears, her mother always said.

April knew her stage because her mother was always telling her about it: letting your glasses slip down your nose and not having enough pride in your appearance to feel them there and push them up!

This was aggravation, but Margery's was more hunched over shoulders at dinner and sighing. "Who's sighing?" her father would say. He liked Margery—quiet and small and took after his side of the family. April thought she saw a little moustache like the one Grandma Flanaghan had before she died, but she just looked, she didn't blurt it out like they said she did.

It was last Christmas Margery got the record player. She begged for it. Next thing was get involved with boys, April didn't want to get involved with boys. "I hope you're not getting started," she heard her mother tell Margery when someone told her how they'd seen kids in the upper grades hanging around at the grill, and boys too.

Margery had already gotten started. April saw her there with Susan Doherty. They sat in a booth all by themselves and each with a box of French fries. They weren't even talking to each other. April watched a good five minutes.

When April got home—she had dawdled—Margery was doing homework on the kitchen table, using one of the ballpoint pens their father was always bringing home from work: Studio Jewelry—this one was blue bottom, pink top. "Hey, I saw you and Susan whatser-name—Doherty this aft," April said. She dropped her schoolbag on the floor so she could pull up her socks. Her mother had sewn her some white elastic garters so she wouldn't be "tugging the G.D. socks all the time," but they didn't work.

Margery didn't look up; she was writing in a tiny, left-slanting script that April loved. She didn't try to imitate it anymore. No matter how much she tried for small letters, they always got bigger and bigger as she went down the page. It looked stupid, plus the penmanship nun always criticized. Her father said Margery must have to concentrate all the time on keeping it small because they were a family of big writers. He printed, but his capitals were very large. Her mother wrote in large, thin letters slanted to the right; when she wrote her name, she sometimes added a wavy line underneath. April tried it; the penmanship nun circled it in red and wrote "refrain" in the margin.

In the third grade she noticed the nuns used small letters to abbreviate their order, Faithful Friends of Jesus (f.f.J.); everyone else was supposed to use capitals. April knew she wanted to be a nun. "Not meaning any disrespect," she told Mother Joseph Magdalen, who called her into the principal's office to ask her the meaning of this. How many times taught the proper way and the reasons she had deliberately disobeyed. The nun was holding the spelling paper April had written the day before with Mother Mary John f.f.J. up in the

9

right-hand corner. It was underlined twice in red. April was surprised they were so mad about it. She told her mother that she couldn't think what to say as an excuse so she said it had "completely slipped" her mind. "Why do you have to pull stunts like this?" her mother said quietly—not in a slapping voice. "Are you listening to me?" she said. April was listening; her mother said what she always said; sometimes she put her face right into April's: think, think, think before you do something!

April *had* thought, but she didn't want to talk back. Her mother wrote a short note in the tall skinny writing on a piece of lined notepaper, the kind she used for the milkman, April began peeling a tangerine, three sentences and "respectfully yours." "Ma?" she said, wanting to tell her to refrain from underlining with the wavy line. "What now?" she said with the slapping voice. "Nothing." Her mother signed the letter, Evelyn M. Flanaghan with the line underneath, and wrote the principal's name on top: Mother Joseph Magdalen, with a sharp line under it. They would be mad, April thought. Her mother had worked herself up. "Where do you think you're going, little girl?" she yelled when April got to the foot of the stairs. "Nowhere." "Get back here till I tell you you can go." April stood near the table until her mother had addressed the envelope, sealed it and held it out to her.

"Take it. And don't you dare grin at me or I'll slap that grin right off your face, you little clown. You like making a fool of us in front of them, don't you? I'd've thought you'd know better by now." Her mother was taking her side for once. She *did* know better, that's what her mother hated: if you try and do something nice, make damn sure it *is* something nice in the first place.

April took the letter and put it in her arithmetic book. Her mother was right behind her. "And don't forget to give it to them, smart-aleck." She gave April a hard little push.

Margery waited for April to pull up her socks so she could ignore her right to her face. She dotted the last *i* in her sentence and then looked over the paragraph, using her little finger, for other places where she could put in some punctuation. "Ma," April called—her mother was

sitting on the hassock in the den, looking through an old magazine—
"Margery won't say hi to me."

"I did too say hi," Margery yelled, "she just didn't hear me. Liar."

Everybody knew Margery hated trouble. Their mother was just
about to get up and start cracking them when Margery jumped out of
her chair, the one with the pad on the seat—her chair was the only
padded one because she was small and needed it to sit up straight—
closed the themebook, grabbed her books, pencil case and package of
Kleenex and ran up the stairs.

"What did you do?" her mother said. "Nothing," April said; her
glasses had slipped off her face and were hanging by one bow, she
pushed them up. "She can't stand me."

"Don't be an actress," her mother said, following her into the den.

"I didn't say anything. I just said I saw her this aft with Susan
Doherty."

"So?"

"At the grill. And then she went berserk."

"I bet you said something else."

"She hates my guts."

April went to make herself half a peanut butter sandwich. A whole
one was too much before dinner, her mother told her every single
afternoon when she started to make it, even though she only wanted
half. If I'm so fat, she said, why don't you just say so?

Don't you talk to me like that.

April ate her peanut butter sandwich on a paper napkin over the
counter and picked up all the crumbs afterward—her mother's eyes
were on her—dropped the paper with the crusts wrapped in it in the
garbage bag, went upstairs. "April," she heard behind her, "what
about the schoolbag? If you think I'm here to pick up after you, you've
got another think coming."

April had seen Margery in there one time before with Susan; it was
a Friday afternoon and they were having a snowstorm. You could
hardly see in the window of the grill because of the steam. The two of
them, sitting in a booth. Nobody sat in a booth; the kids she knew sat
at the fountain where Timmy McNamee, a sophomore in high
school, would razz them; he was a seminarian and "had a way with
people, especially kids," Mr. Feeney, who owned the place, was

always saying. Margery was blowing bubbles in her Coke. April was surprised to see her doing something babyish; she was always telling April not to be a pig gulping down her milk so hard; then their father had to tell them to stop the goddamn bickering. April had never seen her blow bubbles. Her mother was very irritated by little noises. Now she knew where Margery and Susan went.

April dropped the schoolbag on the floor and flopped on the bed, turning the book she had left there right-side up. There was an orphan boy living in a treehouse behind the Appleton place, who was the grandson and real heir of the old lady who had left a fortune but no will, and people thought he was lurking somewhere in town trying to find it, but a fake cousin was trying to get the money another way and the heroine, who decided to try and find the will herself, discovered the empty treehouse. The boy was coming up behind her, thinking she was someone sent from the faker to drive him off his own property. He had a gun in his hand and a rope.

April heard the doorknob squeak, and rolled off the bed so fast there was time to get the uniform jumper half over her head before her mother—who had a feeling the kid would still be in it, the uniform a mass of wrinkles, have to be sent again to the cleaners, only half the year out, and did she think they were made of money?—could see it. But April already had it off. "I'm doing it."

"My eye," the mother said, yanking it over April's head. She handed the jumper back so April could put it on a hanger herself. This one would take advantage of a saint, liked to think her mother was her servant. April stepped into the closet to pull her play pants on quickly before her mother noticed she had her good petticoat on, but her mother had already seen it. She decided to ignore it this time. "Open the window, it smells like a den in here." April, still in the closet, picked up a red cardigan from the floor and put it on to cover the top of the petticoat. She had stuffed the bottom into play pants. She came out of the closet with the sweater nearly buttoned. "What's the matter, no blood in your veins?"

"It's *freezing* in here," April said.

"Shut up," they heard from the next room, "I can't hear myself think." (April laughed at the little voice coming through the wall.)

"Come straight downstairs as soon as you're done picking up this mess. And tell Miss to come down too."

12

Neither of them was allowed in Margery's room without an invitation, and they never got one. The mother would barge in on April whether she liked it or not, but she never did that to Margery, even after April offered to show her how to use a paperclip in the lock. "I don't like to sneak," she had said. Even when she did get in there, she never stayed and got involved like she did in April's room. What kills me, she was always saying, is how closed-mouthed she is. If you want to know something, don't ask that one; she wouldn't tell you to save your life. April thought she should have forced Margery to talk, but her mother told her to mind her own business. "You're no bargain either; don't think you are."

April finished dressing, but she stayed behind a few minutes to see if she had forgotten anything. The uniform belt was visible on the floor until she kicked it into the closet. She rebuttoned her sweater to find a place for the extra button open in the middle where the petticoat showed through, and then tied her shoes. The book was still open on the bed and she read down the page to where he put down the gun; the heroine kept her wits about her through the whole ordeal, not even knowing it was a toy gun or that the boy was the real heir and not a dangerous tramp.

On the way down the hallway, she knocked on Margery's door, yelled into the keyhole; "Fail, fail, gingerale, stick your head in the garbage pail."

One night Margery told their father, who was always telling them how much faith he had in a good education for girls, that she was going to take her high school entrance exam in a month and would need peace and quiet to study for it. "She's not studying in there," April said right away, "she's playing records." Her father told April not to get out of line. The next night he brought home a whole box of pens for Margery and a hardcover desk dictionary. "Study hard," he said. He had slipped a couple of packs of lifesavers in there too, but they were the lousy peppermint kind, so April didn't want any. "Fail, fail, gingerale," she started up again, but was drowned out by "Sixteen Candles" turned up as high as the little record player would go; she blocked her ears to keep from going deaf. Their mother was screaming at the foot of the stairs to turn the goddamn thing down. "I didn't do anything," April yelled back. "Yeah, you never do anything," her mother said.

"Who's this Susan Doherty?" a few minutes later, turning down the TV set so April (Ma!) couldn't hear. "Listen to me," she said. "I am listening," April said, but her mother could see her eyes shifting back to the screen, so she went and stood in front of it. "You can just pay attention to *me* for one minute," she said, holding a potato in one hand and the potato peeler in the other, which struck April as funny, but not so funny she might laugh out loud, just enough to smile, usually enough to aggravate, but not this time. She just turned the set off. She wanted April to get to the point before Margery came down to watch "Donna Reed" at four-thirty. "I don't know," April said, holding onto the sideflaps of the hassock and rocking it from side to side.

"Don't do that. You'll break the spines."

"Spines?" rocking once more to see if she could feel them. There was something rustling in there.

"Is she from school?" working on the potato.

"Yeah, she's in Margaret Mary's homeroom. She's not a bit like Margery, she's smart. They have her say the prayers on First Friday in front of the whole school, she's so smart. You know how we have patrol lines at recess, well—"

"Where does she come from? I've never heard the name. When did she and Margery get so thick?"

"They've been friends a long time," rocking a little, hearing a little crackling sound and rolling the hassock over to look under it. "What's a spine?"

"Since when, I want to know?"

"A year at least, I don't know," rolling the hassock upright and sitting on the armchair with her feet up on it.

"It's all news to me," turning to look in the direction of the stairs. "What were they doing at the grill?" standing up, forgetting the potato which dropped onto the braided rug and rolled under the TV, where April went for it, turning it over in one hand to see what happened to it.

"Will it have a black and blue like an apple?"

"I don't know. Why don't you peel one and see what it has? Are they chasing boys?"

They heard Margery on the stairs. The mother took the potato.

14

"Do you have to walk so heavy on your feet, Margery? You sound like an elephant." Margery kept coming, no change.

"Is the right channel on?"

April turned the TV on again and the two girls settled in the armchairs, April with her feet crossed on the hassock.

"Well, would you look at the ladies of leisure," still holding the potato.

"We'll set the table at the commercial," April said.

Their mother went into the kitchen. "I hate these shows you watch," she said. She carried a pot of water into the den with a newspaper for the peelings and sat down on the hassock right in front of April. "Ma!"

"Move to another chair. I'm working, you're just sitting."

April sighed, moved to the couch next to Margery's chair.

"Don't sit so close to me," Margery said, "move over."

"Stop fighting, you," and the commercial was over, "Donna Reed" on the screen.

As the show was ending they heard the car pull into the driveway, all jumped up. The mother turned the lights on, Margery ran to the kitchen for plates, April carried the peelings in the newspaper and ran back, just as their father was on the porch steps, to turn the TV off. Their father hated the set on in the afternoon.

––––––––

When supper was over and they told their father twice that nothing was new, he asked again. April was carrying four milk glasses to the counter. Margery and her mother were watching. April made it, and then one of the glasses tipped over, milk spilled down the counter and over the side.

"Don't use the dishcloth," her mother said.

April wiped the counter with a napkin, but forgot the little puddle on the floor. "She never finishes anything she starts," her mother said. "April," her father said, but he couldn't see from where he was what the problem was, "I'm warning you."

The three of them, Margery, April and their mother, were so busy with the dishes, making sure no one was getting out of it, that no one had time to tell him what was new; nothing was new. He sat at the table and waited until it was completely clear. April said she'd get the paper for him. While she was in the den gathering it up, he asked Margery how she was doing in her studies.

"Okay."

"Are you getting good use out of the dictionary?"

"Yup."

"When is it?"

Margery had to think; the homeroom nun had said—"Margery," her mother said, seeing the girl had stopped scouring the pans, "can't you think and work at the same time"—Monday week.

"I was talking, Evelyn," the father said.

"Well I've been stuck in this kitchen all day and I'd like to get finished so I can sit and relax like everyone else." Margery gave her a look her mother turned around fast to see and missed.

Margery forgot what they meant by Monday week; they said it all the time: was it this week or next? Had to be this. She turned around to say, but he was reading the paper.

"I didn't hear you tell your father when the test was."

"Monday."

Margery washed the last pot; there was a burn spot on the bottom and her mother handed her the can of Ajax. April was back, and Margery didn't want her involved. It was enough they were all involved. Susan talked for three weeks about the test, and how they had to get into St. Mary's together. Margery didn't think she was going to make it. The nuns had given two sample tests and Margery didn't finish either one. I got nervous, she told Susan, and I couldn't concentrate. They had a different nun in the room, not the homeroom nun whom Margery got along with for a change, patrolling the aisles and writing the time on the blackboard. It was recess and she could hear the little kids playing in the schoolyard. What wrecked the second test was when she noticed the girl across was on the last page and she was only on page two. The nun saw her put her head down on the desk and came right down the aisle. "Oh, get along with you," she said, "don't be a little baby"—"bearbee" was how she said it. All the kids turned to look. The nun found Margery a paper napkin from Gala day last summer to wipe her nose with and asked her if she wanted to go to the basement for a drink. "Well, settle down then; you have"—she spoke up so they all could hear—"eight

16

and a half minutes to finish this section." When she put away her stopwatch, she looked at Margery's answer sheet. "Oh no, Miss," clucking her tongue, "you didn't listen. You're not blacking the holes enough. Push on your pencil like you were told." The nun picked up Margery's neighbor's paper to show her, but Margery couldn't see, she was shaking the paper so hard. "You didn't listen."

Margery used her time to fill the holes in the answer sheet. When she came to answer 15, she noticed she had blacked in two spaces instead of one, using up the answer to the next question, and making that one wrong too. Everything after that was in the wrong space. She put her head down on the desk, but the nun didn't have time for shenanigans; there was half a minute left and she held the bell in her hand and kept her eye on the watch. The proctors—Susan was one—were told to collect the sheets and pass out the new section. Margery looked up when the starting signal was given; all the heads went down together; the nun put her finger on her lips.

They were never that hard at the beginning and she was all right until she got to the reading comprehension and couldn't do the first one about the pigeons changing color near a factory, and then changing back again when the factory moved. She could understand that part, but the questions didn't make any sense. She went back to the beginning to make sure the holes she filled in were good and black. When that was done, she remembered next month would be her birthday and she'd be old enough, they said, to go on a date, if she didn't stay back or fail more than two subjects. Not in cars, but up to the Creamery maybe for a Coke float on a Saturday. In high school they had boy-girl dances Friday nights except for Lent. Even if you do get bored, she told Susan, who hated boys, they could always go downstairs to the cafeteria and get a Coke. Big deal, said Susan, but maybe she'd go if Margery let her talk all she wanted. You'll talk my ear off, she told Susan all the time, just the way her mother would say it. How do your ears feel? Susan said to get back, but she talked just as much. Margery didn't understand how Susan could get worked up over every little thing. It must have been because the family got *Time* magazine and she always had her nose in it. Margery had tried to talk like Susan once at the dinner table. Her father got all upset until her mother butted in and said that when "your father and I are interested in your opinion, we'll ask you." Margery was sorry she had said anything; it wasn't worth it. And all she had done was repeat exactly what Susan had said the day before: that Jackie O'Toole's (the mayor's) construction business had not suffered since he'd taken office, and now the papers were saying his assistant, Ed Curran, a cousin once-removed of Mrs. Dooley's husband, was on the payroll there. It would be one thing (Margery knew she was saying it wrong; when Susan said it it was funny) if this was hush-hush, but everybody and his uncle knew it, and nobody—"That's enough, Margery," her mother said, and changed the subject right away. April came in her room that night and asked how she knew that about the mayor, but Margery, who knew she was just trying to get in good with her so she could listen to a record, told April to get herself right out and stay out.

———

The nuns had said it was impossible to study for the test; it was based, they said, on what you learned way back in grade one and you either knew it or you didn't. Margery lined up all her dolls against the head of the bed; she took her brush and comb and tried to fix up the old baby doll whose top hair had fallen out. Then turned the light on and got a glass of water and the small doll curlers to fix the straggly ends. The long-playing Hawaiian record was on, April could hear it; Margery forgot to turn it down.

———

The nun wrote ⑮ on the board and Margery tried to read the one about the pigeons again; then she tried the next one, the Gross National Product in three Western European countries. It had a graph and two of the questions were about the graph. She looked at the questions, but you couldn't really get them without the story. She knew she was wasting too much time on that one, and skipped down to the next, about the problem of evil in *Moby Dick;* they hadn't read that yet in grade eight, but she had seen part of it on TV. April was watching it, but it was so boring, Margery read a magazine instead. She looked down to question one, then back to the paragraph; it was right there: the whale. The next question must be in the next sentence, but it wasn't; it wasn't in the sentence after that either. There was something about it in the first sentence, but nothing about

18

the first sentence in the choices. There it was: e., None of the Above. She picked e. and moved to the next section. The bell rang for the ten o'clock prayer and the nun said she would stop the clock so they could all stand up and pray. They turned to the statue of St. Theresa, the patron saint of their homeroom, and prayed that Blessed Mary Madeleine Gahagan, who founded the order and only needed one more miracle to become a saint, would get it. It only took two minutes, the nun said, but then the principal came over the radio and they all closed their test booklets and folded their hands. The principal said attendance at the Holy Hour Friday was obligatory, and asked the pupils of Holy Savior School to offer up their prayers for the eighth graders taking their high school entrance examinations Monday week. The principal's bell went off and Mother Fidelis told the children to take up their pencils when the second hand came to twelve. "Ready . . . begin!" She walked to the blackboard and wrote ⑥. "If you have completed your answer sheet," she said, reading from the test jacket a minute later, "check your answers (she paused), and then close the test booklet." Margery decided to check her answers and then, if there were time, start the reading comprehension again. In four minutes, she changed a few more answers to e. because the old answers didn't seem right anymore. Time was up and it was just as well because she was thinking about changing a few more. Leave it be, her mother would say, just leave it be.

Evelyn Flanaghan knew that her oldest wasn't a student. They didn't have to tell her; she could see it at home: she was slow, she didn't use her head, she forgot the thing she had just this minute been told. Still the mother felt if she would try a little harder, she could plug along with the rest of them, but Margery was not a plugger. She gave up too easy, takes after his side, she had said many a time: they don't push themselves either, settle for what they've got, and what have they got? Nothing. There had been talk about repeating fourth grade, but she had gone down to the school herself to have a talk with the fourth-grade nun. She gave the nun her word that she would check the girl's homework every night to make sure she was following what was going on in class, and maybe even to get her a tutor for the summer. "She doesn't tell me or the father anything," Mrs. Flanaghan said, glad to be telling somebody, "so we never know. But I can promise you this, Mother; that girl is going to work, work, work, until she gets it." The nun told Mrs. Flanaghan she was glad to hear it, and wished some of the other parents would take more of an active interest in their children. "We've got a few more like Margery—and don't get me wrong; Margery is a lovely girl—all her teachers say that—but we have no choice but to keep them back if they can't do long division. *We* can't do it for them."

You'll get it if I have to beat it into you every day, April and her father must have heard a thousand times while they were in there watching TV. Margery had to do all her homework downstairs so her mother could keep an eye on her. She had to write her assignments in a little memo book and her mother would read aloud each item and check it off. And every night it was the same song and dance, their father said: Margery would sit down after supper dishes with a face on her a mile long, as their mother said, and start her homework, begrudging every minute of it. Don't even think about watching that television until every bit of that is done, and done to my satisfaction, April and her father would hear. Margery sat under the overhead light doing a set of long divisions, holding the pencil as if it were burning her hand. You can't even hold the pencil right, they could hear the mother say. Press the paper harder, I can hardly read this it's so pale. Get a little life into you. Mrs. Flanaghan would sit and watch TV, going back to the kitchen at commercials to check. They had a blow-out one night when Margery, "planking herself," in front of the television, announced that, because of a feast day, they had no homework.

"You mean to tell me," her mother said in the voice that April knew meant trouble, "here you are a big girl in the fourth grade and failing all your subjects and you can sit there and tell me you have no homework? Get out in the kitchen before your father takes the strap to you and I'm not going to stop him," Mrs. Flanaghan said, following Margery to the stairs where the girl ran.

Another night Margery was sulking and that worked her mother up. She stood shaking the girl's chair until the father, hearing the racket while he and April were trying to watch Phil Silvers, had to tell her to let up.

"You're going to side with her, aren't you? You who don't (the mother) lift a finger around here to help the poor girl out." Now she was going to start on him, even though April—who had come out to the kitchen, too—could see Margery hadn't even opened her book yet. "Who's the one that's been out here every night of the week trying to pound sense into her head?" Margery got up out of her chair saying she had to get a tissue because her hands were sweaty. "*You*," her mother said, "sit yourself down. You like being dumb, don't you? You'd like to spend the rest of your life being dumb and letting other people do your work for you. I've got a good mind to wash my hands of you."

"Take it easy, Evelyn."

"And you keep out of it until you're willing to do the sitting with the girl night after night with no thanks from anyone."

Margery was sent to bed. April thought she was going to get to stay up alone, but she was sent right up, too. "You're no better. Why don't you help your sister if you're so smart?" April was going to say she hadn't done anything, so why yell at her, but she decided not to.

The next night Mr. Flanaghan brought home a box of pencils—not company pencils, but ones he had bought at the dime store, in different colors—and three lined pads. "Thanks," Margery said (it was the first word anyone had heard from her since the night before), carrying them up to her room. That night she sharpened one new pencil and copied her long division onto the new pad. Her mother used another one of the pencils to check her answers. Eight out of ten were right and her mother sent the father right down to the Creamery to buy a quart of peppermint stick ice cream and hot fudge sauce.

"See," she said when he was gone, "you can do it. You can do it if you will only put your mind to it. Now will you put your mind to it?" Margery, who was still copying the corrected problems, nodded. "*Will* you?"

She got a two-week trial period after this when she was allowed to do her homework upstairs without supervision. At the end of the two weeks, Mrs. Flanaghan and Margery had a little talk after supper. Her mother asked how she was doing and she said fine.

"We'll see. We'll send *her* to camp, you know, and you'll go to summer school if you're lying."

"I know."

"You *don't* know."

Providence, 1956: Toy Box

Deliberately, she set down one doll curler on the table. There were three doll curlers, pink and pliable with holes punctured to let the air—she told her friend Ink—get into the curl because that's what curls hair, the air going in and out. The other two curlers were on the couch with the doll comb and a package of cherry cough drops. The doll was on the table, the operating table, she told Ink, sometimes a coffee table: don't spill. The doll, Ina, was face down and she was holding a coil of bright brown hair in her fingers, already so tightly curled that it was hard to roll it smoothly on the tiny rod, but necessary to do so. There was also a cup of water to tame the hair and she wet her fingers and sprinkled water on the doll's head. She's crying, stop that crying, crybaby. She gave the doll a slap and the curler fell out. This was terrible, so she sat on the couch next to the curlers and took Ina on her lap to tell her a story and change the subject. One of the curlers rolled into the crack at the back of the couch and that meant one more lost, stupid; she put one lip over the other, rocking Ina and patting her.

Outside it was snowing, or it could be. The air was dark and the ground looked like snow and the window felt like snow. Any minute. She thought of a story to tell Ina about the snow coming. First it was just a little snow, then it folded over the grass and came up the gutter and flew up a tree and came in the window and went up the chimney until you could walk out the second story window on a mat of pure white snow and the treetops were like flowers or stumps. You could look down the chimneys and climb into the bell tower, slide down to the church floor, and snow there. It never stopped. You'd be so cold, she told Ina, you'd be like a penguin, flapping down the street with the other penguins and Ink would fly away till it was Easter Sunday. And—but she couldn't think of what would happen next so she put Ina down on the couch and pulled Ink over, a black bean bag, and put Ink on Ina's head. Then she used the stand-up ashtray, a round clear ashtray on a metal stand, as a microphone. Ladies and gentlemen, Kukla, Fran and Ollie. Are you ready?

Someone was coming into the room and she let go of the microphone and asked her mother if it was snowing yet. Someone went out of the room. No, she said to Ina, you little ninny, you may not go out. You will stay right in here and do as you're told. She picked up the bean bag and left Ina on the couch crying.

Friday, it was Friday. Was it Friday? The calendar was over by the washing machine and you had to find the day by letter. There was a circle around one of the days and a message next to one of the days. She lifted the pages standing tiptoe to find December, one page away, and the calendar was over. The picture on the calendar was Jesus pointing a finger to his heart which had a flame over it and a little cross. She knew his pain was there because the heart was not inside the skin but outside. Sacred Heart of Jesus. What are you doing with that? Did you leave your toys in the parlor? You did. Go pick them up and don't be a little slob. He had a white shirt on and a red cloak. I'm going.

———

Ina's head came off if you pulled at it, but there was nothing inside. It was smooth inside and it smelled nice like powder. The bean bag smelled nice too, ink ink, a bottle of ink. Mary? Cap fell off and you stink. What? Come in here and help me make the supper. She didn't know what to do with Ina. But in the meantime, Ina's head would not go back on and she had made the mistake of putting Ink down in there, and now she couldn't get it out. Can you hear me? Nothing to do but put all the things together, put the curlers in there, two of them, the bobby pin she found on the rug and cough drops, and carry the head and body, run, so no one would see. Where are you going?

A my name is Alice, my husband's name is Al. She opened her window to see if it was snowing and up there in the sky was the snow, you could see it, but it wasn't falling. The sky was full of it, and there was Mary Madeleine Burke behind her garage hiding. Hey girlie, she said, but not loud enough, gir—lie, that was almost loud enough, but Mary Madeleine, who had climbed the fence and was dangling her head over the other side, couldn't hear. Hey, you deaf or something? She heard, "hi, Mary." Hi, Mary Madeleine. "My name isn't Mary Madeleine." Yes it is so.

Mary, you get down here and shut that window. But she couldn't shut it. It was too hard, and Mary Madeleine had run across the street, didn't look both ways and there she was, right under the window. "Can you come out?" No. "Why?" Go back home, get off my property. "Says who?" Says my father. "Yeah?" I'll see if I can come out; my doll is broken. "I have two dolls." Okay, go home and get your baby carriage. "My baby carriage is broken." Not it is not. "Yes, it is so, my brother got in it and it broke." Why don't you fix it? The window was being shut from behind and she was getting a good shaking from her mother. Sometimes her tongue would get caught in her teeth and bleed. This time, it was free and just in the middle. It was shaking in there and then the shaking stopped. When it stopped, she could see that Mary Madeleine had run home. Now are you going to mind me? Are you?

———

You're a stupid girl, she told Ina that night, a dumb ox and a baby. Ina was still broken, but no one had seen. First she put Ina in the corner to be fixed, with the head just resting on top; but later, after dumping all the things on the bed, she put the two parts deep in the toy box under the gumball machine and in the baby blanket. When she was wrapping the parts in the baby blanket, she found the poppet beads she couldn't find last time—they were down in a corner—and unpopped them to fit them around her neck. Once she had gone to the bathroom in this box, but that was forgotten, plus the poppet beads, pink, were new. You could keep adding to them by going down to the dime store and buying a new chain. She climbed on top of the toy box and sat there with the poppet necklace around her neck and part of it in her mouth. Pretty soon, her mother would call, go home, your mother's calling you, but there was a little time to rest.

24

It still wasn't snowing, but now it was dark and you couldn't tell. The streetlight looked like snow, but it wasn't. My mother and your mother were hanging out the clothes. She heard someone in the bathroom. My mother gave your mother a punch in the nose. Still in there. What color was the blood?

Today they had made an apple pie and a small pie which Mary could share with her dolls and toys at the small table and chairs in the cellar where her house was. Her mother carried the little pie in a dishtowel, but it was still very hot. Mary went up stairs to get the family. She came down with the bean bag and a paper doll, Blue Bill. Where's your doll? Her mother walked down the cellar stairs right behind her, carrying the tray of pink cups and the pink water pitcher filled with water for the tea party. I thought Ina was your best friend. Mary put Blue Bill on a chair and Ink on a chair. I'm talking to you. Maybe she is, maybe she isn't. Mary sat on the one chair with balloons painted on it, a white chair with balloons of different sizes, and her mother pulled up an old kitchen stool. Out of her apron pocket came two folded-up napkins which she unfolded and placed on the table in front of Mary and herself. Is it snowing? How should I know? They ate the pie, but it was too hot and Mary had a burn spot on her tongue; she could still feel it. Her mother wanted to know what in God's name happened to your doll, I don't understand you, go get it and bring it to me, I think you broke it.

After the tea party, they carried the dishes upstairs and Mary took the two guests to her room while her mother rinsed the little dishes and put them on the stairs to be packed in their own chest, which was an old toy box of her mother's. Mary didn't know how she could fit all her toys in it, but that's what she said. Her father made it when she was a little girl. It was wood and had splinters in it and a small metal handle like a tool box. Her mother said she could use it, but not to break it or throw it away.

Her door was opening. Why are you sitting there doing nothing? Aren't you supposed to be getting ready for bed? What did I just tell you? Her mother sat down on the bed. Mary slid off the toy box and circled the room, keeping close to the walls in case she was going to catch it, slid into the closet where her nightie was on the floor over the shoes, smelled funny in there, sat down—you can undress in front of me, I've seen you before—and unbuckled her shoes. She was taking forever, and soon her mother opened the closet door, pulled her by the arm, yanked the jersey over her head without even unbuttoning the sweater that was over it. You're hurting me. She lifted her up and sat her on the bed, pulled off the overalls and a shoe; the other shoe fell off and a sock. Look at the mess you're making. Mary was shivering on the bed in just an undershirt (her mother called it a shirttail; her father called it an undershirt; her grandmother called it a chemise) and underpants, and now the flowered flannel nightie was over her head, and her head was too big. Where'd you get such a big head? There—and now she was pulled into the bathroom and sat on the rim of the tub to have her face and hands rubbed with the face cloth and soap. Don't get it in my mouth. Sometimes the soap didn't rinse off and Mary could taste it in the night and gag. Then prayers. Did you say them? I didn't hear them. Say them again. I already said them silently. Say them again. Say them so I can hear them. Not there, kneel down like the sisters say. Are your eyes closed? Mary could see through her eyes closed that her mother wasn't looking. She was watching something, or listening for something. I can't hear. Say them louder.

————

Mrs. Mary F. Fatso McGillicuddy, hundred years old, was in grade two, Holy Savior School ("Save-Your," her father said; the nuns always said "The School of the Holy Savior"; her mother said "school"; and Nana said the "sister school") with a big bee-hind, and learning how to use fountain pen with the inkwell. They didn't fill the inkwell like they should have. They filled our inkwells when I was a little girl, her mother said. All day long, when Mary was in grade one, Mother Anna, she played with the lid of the inkwell, slid back and forth over the hole. Sometimes the desks just had a hole; this one had the inkwell in it. But they were using ink bottles now. She had an ink bottle; royal blue in a square bottle with bumps on it, inside was the ink, watery and easy to spill just by tipping. The ink pen was black and you had to dip it just so and not put a puddle of ink anywhere on the page or on the desk. Sometimes a little ink would get on the sleeves of the uniform blouse, but that was because she had no sleeve guards. She forgot to ask her mother for the money and the nuns had told her time and again: shocking—And where are the sleeve guards you were told to buy and told how many times, Miss? So the blouse had a little ink on the cuffs, but no ink on the page. She was copying in a beautiful hand—And what do you call that? Look what you're doing, you little silly . . .

All men, at the moment of death and in death's final agony, must wait in trembling expectation for the judgment of Almighty God, their Father. Do not wait, my children, but know the multitude and qualities of your sins and offenses. Make your soul a golden chalice of purity so the blood of the Lamb, your Savior, may flow into it, and overflow its gleaming sides.

That was that, a nice period, a dot just like that, and holding it just a minute, it was a blot and oh no, traveling in little thin lines around the blot and still the nib right there in that little pool of ink. Now there was a hole in the paper, just a little hole from pressing so hard, a mistake, and pulling the pen out of the hole, there was a cut in the paper and ink, more of it than you'd think, making a flow of light blue like a cloud across the perfect letters and then the letters becoming clouds in the cloud. She looked up but nobody was there just yet. There was time. So she lifted an edge of the thin sheet and the free ink ran fast from one side, then to the other, yet was held in the paper like the paper was a dish. Her eyes started to fill with water long before the nun reached her desk, before she even saw her get started and jump from her desk to swoop down, as her mother would say, on the girl who was deliberately disobeying; she felt them fill and was afraid, and there was still time so she let the ink, its beautiful thin blue curtain, fall on the top of the desk and fast down the slope into her lap, which was also blue, so it didn't matter, or maybe it did. Her legs were a little wet and this was like an accident. Now she was laughing and could feel the water in her eyes overflow like pins onto her cheeks and then really starting up so that the nun, reaching the desk, a black furious cloud and rolling down the gulley faster and faster, saw the eyes in the nick of time and the slap she was going to get right in the face, stopped. The whole class would be crying, the nun too, before long.

Stayed Back

Margery didn't go to summer school, April didn't go to camp. They had said: if you can't send one, you can't send the other, but there were other reasons. Things started happening right at the end of school. First, nothing happened. They put wrapping paper on the books and washed the desks, there was a day of recollection and one whole day spent putting lines on spelling paper. Most of the day was just sitting. Promotion day was like that. They sat in "full uniform" with their hands folded from 8:00 on, waiting for the monsignor to come, and some years he didn't come until right before lunch. He always told a joke first thing and said they should try and guess the punchline if they could. Last year a girl in Margery's class got it. She didn't get in trouble, Margery said; he just changed the subject and started calling the names.

The monsignor liked to make fun of the names—not all the names, just the Irish ones. The Italian ones he didn't bother, April figured, because they were already funny. April's mother couldn't stand the pastor (she still called him the pastor; everyone else switched to monsignor as soon as he was promoted) because right in the middle of the Mass, he'd turn around to scream at the men standing in the back of the church to come up to the front and sit down. This was embarrassing, she said, plus it gave scandal that a priest would have such a temper. But April felt he made up for it at times like this when things got so funny, even the nun grinned, and they were always serious on promotion day.

The ones who weren't promoted didn't cry right away. The nuns made them all turn their cards face down on the desk, stand up, good morning Msgr. Fahey, sit down, hold their tongue until he was gone. Somebody always cried. The nuns would send them down to the basement for a drink. They wouldn't really start crying until they were let out and started home. April had seen this happen.

Cried in the schoolyard and kept it up all the way down River Avenue. A lady coming out of the A&P stopped to ask if she were lost.

Didn't step on any cracks in front of the dentist's office. No one in grade two did. Her knee socks were falling down and this (April) would only make matters worse at home. The kid let up a little when she went around the corner and up Maple Avenue. April stopped at the newsstand to smell the cigars. By that time, the kid was already in the five and ten.

April knew her—Patty Curran, one of the Currans—Margery had one of them in her room too. See the whole family on Sunday going up to communion together, all except the father, who worked out of state and was hardly ever home. "No love lost there," April's mother said. "A pillar of the church," is what April's father *always* said as soon as Mrs. Curran's name came up; no need—he'd known Mrs. his whole life—to slander a family like that. The oldest, Jackie, in Margery's grade, was going into the priesthood, and everybody knew it. This was a credit to Mrs. Curran, plus the fact that they (April's father) always speak to you on the street.

In the schoolyard April overheard the first grade nun telling Patty that she was breaking her poor mother's heart. April couldn't see it. Mrs. Curran was a big tall woman, always wore a hat. She had six kids, so what did it matter that one of them was staying back? And none of them paid any attention to little Patty, as April's mother called her. Even in the first grade she went home all by herself, although the rest of them were right there in the upper grades.

If I were her, I'd get right home (April) and face the music. The nun had just that day finished telling them what happened to kids like that. "Some of you won't be back with us in the fall," she said.

They always talked about this subject right before the summer. And, every summer some kid died. A girl in Margery's third grade drowned in the Fanueil Street pool. Another summer, Jackie McDonald was caught under the wheels of the ice-cream truck. "Now what business (Mother Dolores) did that young man have interfering with the ice-cream truck?" When April was in kindergarten, two kids caught polio and never came back, although they weren't dead; they were in the iron lung. "Children have been told (the principal) time and time again not to swim in public places with polio around."

That was a different year, Margery had said afterward; those two kids weren't even *at* the swimming pool. April's mother felt the same way about sitting on the sidewalk playing jacks with the uniform jumper on, but at least you couldn't get killed doing it. Patty Curran, already in terrible trouble, wasn't even waiting for summer to get involved.

April put her lunchbag, with the promotion card in it, on the sidewalk near the curb and went to look in the dime store window. The candy counter was right in front, and there was Patty. She had two Reese Cups in one hand, a roll of Necco wafers and a nickel pack of bubble gum in the other. She gave the lady a quarter. April couldn't see giving that kind of money to a kid staying back. The cashier had to reach way over to give Patty her nickel change.

"You got nose trouble?" Patty said, seeing April there staring.

They hadn't walked one block together when Patty had the Necco wafers open and ate two and April could see she wasn't going to get any. It didn't matter; the black one was way down in the middle.

"I could have got a cherry coke if I wanted," Patty said, when they stopped at the Palace spa to look in the window, "but I just spent my last dollar." To the other stuff she had done, April could see she was going to add lying.

They stopped at the Palace theater. "South Pacific" was coming, but "The Swiss Family Robinsons" was still playing, and April had to look at the snake. "I'm going to have nightmares," she said. So what? "But that's nothing compared to what you're going to get." The candy counter was right there in the middle of the lobby where the cleaning lady was washing the floor. "Peeyu," said Patty, sticking her nose up to the crack between the glass doors. April tried to stick her nose in there too. "Made you look, dirty crook, stole your mother's underhook." Not underhook, under*wear*, stupid.

Patty turned left on Beaufort. April could take this street, or any other street on this side, so she took this street. Patty stopped short in front of the Donavan house, with the two old ladies up on the second floor—one was mental, April's mother said—and started picking red

berries off the hedge. "You better not—they'll call the cops on you."
Patty kept picking. April picked one and looked for somewhere to put
it. "I lost my bag!" she yelled. What bag?

April ran around the corner, and there was an old lady in front of
the dime store, sure enough, tapping at the bag with her cane. "Get
out of there, you." The old lady turning around, not paying the least
attention, walked into the Five and Ten. April ran to the bag. The
promotion card was still there.

When she got back to Beaufort, Patty was sitting on the curbstone
throwing berries down the sewer one by one. What do you got in
there? putting two candies, yellow and black, back to back on her
tongue. "Nothing. My promotion card, see?" You shouldn't keep it
in there, it'll stink. "No, it won't—here, smell it." Patty put her hand
in the bag and pulled out the card. I bet your mother'd kill you if
someone threw this here down the sewer. April took the card back
("I'm not afraid of midgets"). Yeah, ink ink a bottle of ink, the cap
fell off and you stink. "Shut up." Shut up yourself.

––––––

"Ma, I'm home. The screen door didn't slam." Nobody in the
kitchen. She yelled up the stairs, down the cellar stairs and went out
the front door and circled the house. A waste because her mother
didn't like to go outside. "I don't have time for idling. First thing you
know they'll (the neighbor ladies) see me out here and want to come
over and gab."

Inside again, she unpacked the promotion card and set it up against
the sugar bowl, holding it up with a coffee spoon, and a little drop of
coffee right there on the border. Upstairs, no beds made, shades
pulled, a pile of dirty sheets on the bathroom floor. It was like
nighttime. April stood in front of the bureau mirror in her mother's
room and turned the two china-doll lamps on. They had real cloth
dresses and the dust in them made April sneeze.

Make-up all over the top of the bureau. A jar of liquid make-up,
"face stuff" ("Get me my face stuff from the bureau"), her mother
called it. Red thing of rouge with a little powder puff that had rolled
out to the edge of the bureau. A bobby pin had fallen right on it.
Little thing of eyebrow stuff and a brush, box of orange face powder
with the cover off, but the puff still in there and powder all over the

bureau scarf. April put a finger in it. Powder on the mirror too. She took the powder puff and patted her cheeks, but there was too much on it and it fell on the uniform jumper. She took one of the balled-up Kleenexes and rubbed the extra off her cheeks, then stuck a finger in the rouge and put some on each. There were three lipsticks, two had fallen over on the glass plate where the perfume and hairclips were. She found Oh-so-coral and drew some lips the way she had seen her mother do it, with a little finger pointing to the chin. "Oh, look at you (she made a mistake), you're such a clown."

In the bathroom she soaped her mouth to fix it, and the powder and rouge got mixed. She wet a cloth and lay it dripping over her face the way she had seen her do it. Then she went back to try more.

She fixed the streaky places with face stuff, took a look, pinched her cheeks and pulled back her bangs with bobby pins. She pulled out her mother's new birdcage hat from the closet shelf. It was still in a plastic bag with a big ball of tissue paper stuffed into it to keep it round. April unpacked it carefully, but a little powder happened to drop on one of the velvet bows ("Oh, you're so destructive, April"), and it had to be rushed to the bathroom, soaked in a little water, wrung out, rolled up in a towel. It was too bad, it could have looked beautiful, but she put it back, stuffed with the paper, into the plastic bag. The velvet bow was all wrinkled, but it was in the back, no one would notice.

She had just gotten the top drawer open, with the cigar boxes full of jewelry to see if maybe a choker and bracelet might be nice, when there was a noise. It sounded like a box of crayons had dropped. Was that the front door? She ran into the bathroom, locked the door and climbed into the empty hamper. Nothing—no noise—so she unlocked the door and sat back down on the hamper top.

She went downstairs the hard way, holding onto the bannisters with both hands and lifting her feet right off the ground. The bottom step creaked, so she jumped over it and landed hard with heels and taps on the linoleum.

It was too quiet, plus it was dark. She found the newspaper on the parlor floor where the paperboy had thrown it. If you want to kill your father dead, her mother was always saying, all you have to do is leave the goddamned door unlocked so anyone can just walk in and take something. April locked it. The other thing he hated was turn the

32

lights on and leave the blinds open so the neighbors could see in. And all the slats going every which way, but April didn't feel like doing any of it.

At the kitchen table she played with the promotion card, then the Angelus bell rang. She said the Angelus out loud, sitting, even though there was a Sacred Heart plaque up over the door frame she could have stood and looked at. It was way up there because there was nowhere else to put it where it wouldn't be seen, yet it had been blessed and you couldn't throw it out. If there was one thing her mother despised, it was religious art in the downstairs. On the second floor, she didn't mind, and they all had a crucifix over their beds— Margery had a braided palm in hers. April's palm had fallen behind the radiator and gotten all dried out, so she just left it there. This was a sacrilege, she knew; she didn't need Margery to tell her that. "I haven't *disposed* of it, that's the main thing." It was a sin (the nuns) to dispose of it.

Even in the spring they had to build their May altars upstairs in the bedrooms because their mother didn't want them "cluttering" the living room. April made hers with no statue because Margery didn't want her "traipsing into my room every minute of the day" to use *her* statue to pray. April made her own out of an old twirling baton with the rubber caps gone, covering it with a baby doll coat, using a baby blanket for the veil. The blanket was hung low so you couldn't tell there was no face. She tacked blue streamers to the wall and put a bunch of dandelions and a few violets in a vase, along with two roses she had picked out of a neighbor's yard. Margery, the stupid jerk, was so busy making remarks about what a funny statue it was, she didn't even notice. Good thing, because there would have been a terrible beating. If her mother had told her once, she had told her a million times not to pick flowers in other people's yards. And Margery was a tattletale.

Five minutes. The streetlights were on and April couldn't see any kids playing outside. They had all gone home. Why hadn't they waited to go till she came home? Yeah, why didn't they? she said. She decided to go look for them. Were they up the avenue? At the A&P? What if they had taken the bus downtown? She ran to the hallway window to see up the street where the bus stop was.

There was somebody. It looked like the lady across the street, Mrs.

33

Dooley, and the married daughter, Agnes. They were just a block away, but on the other side of the street. That was just a little kid. No, it wasn't. April thought she recognized a red coat. It was too dark, but she was sure that was stupid Margery trying to look like a big shot in her squashed heels and white knee socks, which she got for Easter. "Spindle," her father called her because her legs were like sticks. After church she had to take them right off and coat them with vaseline, put them back in the box they came from because they cost a small fortune and her mother didn't want the kid wrecking them.

April ran out the door just as her father's car was pulling into the driveway. "They're home," she shrilled. "Where are you running off to?" He was carrying a shopping bag full of something, but April didn't have time to find out what. "I'm talking to you. Answer me!" April was almost past the car, panting; "Here they are!" Her mother and Margery were coming up the sidewalk two houses down, with the two sets of heels and faces on them a mile long. April could see Mrs. Dooley looking out her parlor window through a slat in the blind. The dog at the Carey house was yipping. "Get inside that house, you," her father said, giving her a little shove with the bag—there was something hard in there. April wondered if it was a toy truck, that's what it felt like. Who was that for? "Ma!" she yelled, "where'd you go all this time?" Her father right behind her with the hard package. "Did you hear me? Get in there and stop making such a racket out here."

They went in; April kept turning to see if they were following. Margery was last and looked back to show Mrs. Dooley they knew she was there. The slat dropped. Everyone was quiet but April. *They* had the sense, their father said afterward, not to let the whole world know their business. *That one* will never learn, he said.

"What happened to your face?" April screeched the minute she saw her mother in the light. "What happened to *your* face, stupid?" Margery said, giving April a look. "Would you two mind shutting the hell up," their father said, but they all started up again. "Where were you gone to all this time? I was home all by myself." "Do I have to speak to you again, April?" Margery was behind him trying to get a look inside the bag. "Go upstairs," their father yelled. "Go." "I didn't do anything (Margery). Why do I have to go?" "Just do it."

Margery went first since he could only hit the last one, but he didn't hit. Halfway up the stairs they heard the refrigerator door open and someone sit down. Margery squatted down on the stairs and April tried to sit down on the same step but was pushed off. "I don't want you right next to me." Margery took off the good patent leather shoes and put them where April couldn't see them or get a fingermark on them. They sat still, but they didn't hear anything. Then they heard him go into the parlor and shut blinds.

Margery wouldn't tell April no matter how much she begged. "Go wash your dirty face," she said, but April told her she had already washed it with Ajax and it still wouldn't come off. Margery followed April into the bathroom so they could look at it in the mirror. "If they're not telling," she said, "I'm not telling." "Get an apron on," they heard from downstairs, "and start helping."

During supper April tried to get a look at the face, but her mother caught her and told her to stop gawking like a damn fool. It was covered with something pink and the pimples underneath the pink were inky.

It was much later that night when April finally worked it out of Margery for a nickel and the use of her Crayolas. How many months now had her mother's face been like that? She couldn't remember when it wasn't. "What's the matter with your face?" their father was always saying, and that always got something started, so April didn't dare say anything. She didn't even look, if she could help it. Every night her mother stood over the bathroom sink filled with hot water and her face almost in the water, a towel over her head. Then she put Clearasil all over it and went to bed. She always left the bathroom door open, and April sat on the hallway floor and talked. During the day, she had it all covered up with face stuff. "You can still see things," April said once, sitting on her mother's bed watching. "You can't keep that big mouth shut, can you? Did it ever dawn on you that no one's interested in what you have to say?" That was the day they did Easter shopping. There was no good time that day. She wasn't even nice to Margery, who hadn't said anything. "What'd I do?" "Be quiet," the mother said.

Now they knew what it was and why it wasn't going away. It was an infection, not pimples like everybody thought. Now, at least they knew, their mother kept saying to him. The doctor had given her a new prescription for face stuff, plus penicillin and a needle to inject it, and told her to bathe it six times a day in hot hot water. I'm going to learn how to do the shot, Margery said. April couldn't believe it.

That night, even though April yipped at her mother half a dozen times about being left alone in an empty house, and Margery had come home with a provisional promotion to grade five, and their father had bought a rubber potato and onion bin that didn't fit in the spot where their mother kept the potatoes and onions, and how could he have gotten it wrong when she had gone to the trouble of measuring it and giving him the measurements? there were no hard words. For supper they sent out for meatball sandwiches from Ma-nelli's and everyone ate on paper towels so there was no mess and everyone could sit right down after dinner and watch TV.

Their father said—when April and the mother went off in the car to pick up the sandwiches—that he and Margery were going to have to have a little talk about school, but he didn't say it in a temper and they didn't talk after all. The only trouble that got started was when April tried to say how much the face was getting better already; she could see clear places—"mind your own business," her mother said before she even got it all out. She wanted to say *something,* so a few minutes later, she got started about being left all alone in the house again. Her father said if she didn't shut up, he was going to send her up to bed. Then, with all the screaming—because the mother got involved in this conversation—and the trouble of the day, and the fact that the patient on the program they were watching was having a head operation without any ether and was wide awake while they were lowering a big pipe into his head, Margery started to cry, and then they started on her because "it's too late to cry now, you should have cried a long time ago."

But it blew over. Margery ran upstairs to her room and locked herself in. There was talk about whether one of them should go right up there and then and give her a talking to. There was even an idea, April thought, that there was a beating coming to her when things calmed down, but in the end no one got one. "I'm pooped," their mother said at the next commercial. Margery was sitting on the floor again leaning her back against the hassock. *She* had gotten into her mother's make-up too, April noticed. Her lips were orange and there was a little shred of Kleenex sticking to them. Margery saw April looking and gave her a terrible look back and was starting to give a pinch, but April moved out of the way in time. Nothing more was said that night. Their mother went up at ten to bathe her face and Margery went up with her to learn how to give the shot. April was right behind them, until her mother swung around and told the little "pesty ass" to go back downstairs and stay there until she was told to go to bed, or she would go to bed right now.

Twenty minutes later they were all in bed, all except him. April heard the toilet flush and could hear him getting into bed. She could see the light underneath her mother's door. Margery and the mother always shut their doors; April and the father left theirs open. He was listening for fires, but April was afraid to fall asleep with the door shut.

––––––––

Nobody did anything that summer because everything was up in the air. Their mother's face didn't get better, although she was on the phone every day telling her friend Eileen Burke that she could see clearings and how dry it was getting around the nose. But it got worse, not better, and the trouble spread to her neck and back; it was so bad on the neck, it looked like boils. Margery didn't give the shot that good; she was too afraid, so their mother had to do her own shot. Now she always kept the door shut when she was in the bathroom. Finally, she was taken to the hospital for observation. Even when she came home, it wasn't better.

Their father was mad all the time from not getting enough sleep and having bronchitis again; Margery, skinny to start with, lost more weight and started getting pimples herself, which drove their father crazy. He kept telling them to take care of their skin, to keep it clean!

Nobody did anything that summer but wait and see, offer up their masses and prayers and try not to get things started. It was hard because everybody's nerves were on edge and ready to get worked up. April must have had ten beatings and a thousand slaps in the mouth that summer, plus a million remarks, tongue-lashings, naggings, tempers, screams and hard words. It got a little better at the end of the summer and their mother was able to hide it better under make-up, but it never went away and you could always see it.

Providence, 1934:
The House at the Beach

The house isn't there anymore. It was my mother, he said, who loved this house. In those days it had a porch and she would sit there as soon as she got up, and all day long, and into the evening, with all the cousins next door sitting on their porch, all looking out at the water, a narrow strip of bay with no beach at all, just rocks and broken shells. She used to wear bathing shoes made of thin pink rubber, although she said she could still feel the rocks cutting into her feet when she waded up to her ankles or knees.

He could always see her there, her face, coming in from the water, like a white dish above the green bannister of the porch and behind the red rusted screen. She wasn't a well woman and she never went outside, or almost never. She liked to just sit, he said. He said the worst disappointment was when the house blew down in the '38 hurricane. When you hear people tell that story, they always start from where they were when they heard, and work their way back to the house. They found the garage door up the street, but the rest was gone.

It was a white clapboard house with a front room and a kitchen on the first floor and three small bedrooms on the second floor. The family was small, and—although people came to visit from the city during the summer—no one stayed over, plus there were all those cousins next door, so who needed guests?

They always left the day he brought home his promotion card. One year he didn't bring it home, but she was gone by then, the front stoop was in the sea, three feet underwater in high tide. When he brought all the others home, though, small white cards with a thin black border and dashes for his name and grade and the nun's name in blue-black ink, she took them and put them away in the shoebox with all his health records, report cards and messages from the school. The shoebox was on a high shelf in the front-hall closet, next to the hats and scarves that were out of season. She didn't know where to keep it, and was always having to drag it out for one reason or other, without being able to get it back up there again, so it would lay on chairs or on the arm of the sofa for a week or two weeks until someone else got anxious about it and got the stool from the kitchen to put it away safely.

———————

The bags would be all packed and piled up on the back seat of the car. His father had already brought down two loads on the two preceding Sundays, but his mother didn't like to go down there until it was time to stay. Helen loves it down there, his father was always telling people. That's your best time of year, isn't it, Hel?

There were broken rocks all over the beach now; the grass grows to the end of the street, and then there's nothing but rocks and coarse beach sand, and all that time, there were all those rocks and shells right under the house. His mother wouldn't let him play under the house. The house was on stilts like all the other houses and there was a place under there that was shaded and smelled of mildew and seaweed. She must have known, someone said, that it wasn't going to stay that way forever. They don't build houses like that anymore—on stilts—but in those days it was the thing to do, plus you could get very close to the water, if not a little way into the water, at high tide, the way his cousins' house was. All girl cousins and now all married with grown-up children, one already dead. He still had a picture of the cousins all in white sailor suits sitting on the front steps of their house. You could just see their mother's feet; she was sitting in the green wicker rocking chair. There was a picture of him and his sister in sailor suits, too; it was taken in a photographer's studio; it was a very uninteresting picture, he thought; they were sitting side by side and she had an arm around him, their heads tilted toward each other. He didn't remember Eileen so well at the beach house; she was always next door with the cousins, yelling her head off; they were more her

age than his. Can you imagine what it was like, he told his wife, to
have so much family, so many kids right there, that you never had to
go looking for friends? But he did go looking for friends. Every day he
took his bike out of the toolshed and rode three miles down the dirt
road to the amusement park that was out there on the point; beyond
that was nothing but ocean and the lighthouse. He hid his bike in the
sand under the boardwalk—because they had a real beach there—
and would spend the day at the park watching people on the rides and
listening to the music. If he had a nickel, he played a couple of games
of chance on the raffle wheel or went into the penny arcade, or else
he bought a mug of root beer and a ball of cotton candy on a blue
paper cone. Toward the end of summer, he would go more and more,
every day if he could, because the time was going so fast, and soon
they would be moving back. And the beach got so boring; one of the
cousins was always crying; the mothers' faces floating like balloons
behind the screen. He had a raft one year and that kept him
busy—the only boy and the youngest of all. By the time he was old
enough to go into the water by himself, two of his cousins were
already sitting on the porch with the family and drinking iced coffee
or highballs in the summer glasses, which were left there all year long.
War was threatening one year, he remembered, and people were full
of memories; one of the cousins got engaged and wore linen dresses
with white shoes and white silk stockings, which were very popular.
His mother often wore hats, even sitting on the porch. She took to
sitting alone on her porch smoking a cigarette. Next door were his
aunt and uncle and two of the elder cousins. They always seemed to
be having a good time "amongst themselves," as his mother said, and
their voices could be heard up and down the beach.

They thought she had gotten very uppity, but she hadn't, he said;
she was just starting to be ailing. And with Eileen next door all the
time and sometimes staying overnight, it was just the two of them all
the livelong day. His father stayed in the hot city during the week so
he could get to work, and sometimes he stayed there on weekends
too; but mostly, he gassed up the black Ford on Fridays at 4:30 and
drove the fifteen miles to the shore, full of pep he was, with two
quarts of Seagrams in the back and a case of beer; once in a while he
brought a big frosted cake from the bakery.

They could hear the car, his mother and he, coming over the

gravel right up to the line where the rocks and shells began. He would run out of the house, but sometimes one of the cousins and Eileen would get there first. Often his father brought a quarter's worth of bulls' eyes and orange slices and stuck them in pockets or on top of their heads, or on belts or up sleeves, just to be funny. Friday nights they had a nice ham and bean supper for both houses at the cousins'. It was always fun, but sometimes his father drank too much and got rambunctious, and his mother would have an attack. When he didn't, they had games after supper and when it got dark, they all moved to the porch and sang and told stories watching the moon rise over the water. At night it always looked like there was something interesting over on the other side, there where all the lights were blazing, but it was just Bay View, a beach just like theirs, although his mother said there was money over there. That was the summer he had the idea of swimming across. He knew there wasn't money lying right on the streets, but his mother had shown him a war bond she kept in her scarf drawer and he wondered if maybe that's what you'd find over there if you went looking.

Of course, he told his wife, they had more money those years than they ever had. His father owned property in the city and there was also the car; cars were rare, especially in wartime, he said. The cousins never had one. And then there was the beach house, too. As far as he knew, there were only four families in the whole parish who had a summer house, as they called them then.

———

During the night he could hear his mother in the bathroom; he could hear water running and another noise that sounded like somebody was slipping in the tub. When he couldn't sleep, he would creep on his belly across the cold bumpy linoleum of his bedroom, his head just sticking out into the hallway, to listen. He could see the light under the bathroom door and hear water. Some nights he would get himself all worked up: why didn't she just go to bed? Why was it the same thing every night? Once he fell asleep right on the floor, waking up with the cold, the whole house dark, the fog horn blowing and the fog, so thick, it gathered just inside the window and sank all the way down to the floorboards. The air had a salty taste. If he were awake enough, he would creep out of the room on his elbows and work his way down the hallway to just outside her room. Sometimes her light was on, but he knew she liked to sit in the dark. This happened in the city too, but at the beach house it seemed so much worse because the walls were thin, the windows always open and there were no street-lights, just the light from the sky, with the water coming right up to the front porch and the seagulls sleeping in a circle right out there in the middle of the water. Everything was dark and moving. His mother and father slept separately because she had to be up so often. Helen, if you ask me, I think you bring it on yourself, he said. Some nights she didn't get up at all and he liked to point this out to her. It's abnormal, he would say, for a woman your age to have so much trouble sleeping. But even he knew that it wasn't that—sleeplessness; it was nerves. She was very nervous. Her hands shook: when they had soup for lunch, he would have to carry the bowls to the table. She wouldn't eat much and she "always had a face on her," as his father would say. But it wasn't a bad face, or a sick face; in fact, he didn't think it was anything but his mother's face; she told him she always tried to have a little prayer on her lips and that's how she looked: her lips chapped and parted, moving every once in a while, her fingers on the rosary she kept in her pocketbook. It was a face of prayer; his mother was never one for idle chat, and in the years before she died, she said very little at all. But she did—and everybody knew this—she did like to come down to the beach; in fact, it was one of the greatest pleasures of her life.

His father, who owned a construction business with his brothers, was a short man with moustaches. He walked with a cane and liked to dress up. In the old days his mother would tease his father about being so fussy with his shirts and shoes. They would sit down together of a Saturday night with all his father's shoes laid out in a row and his baby shoes next to them. He had one pair of high baby shoes, brown leather. His father had a shoebox full of polish cans; some of the cans only contained a rim of polish, but his father rubbed at the rim with a stained old diaper until there was nothing there at all, and still he put the can back in the box when he was finished. His father told him once he had made a mistake buying a can of blue polish, for he only owned the one pair of blue shoes and wore them, at most, three times a season, and the polish was going to waste. When he was six, his mother gave in and bought him a pair of blue shoes, but by then the polish had dried up and cracked, although his father had done everything he could to make it soft again; they pounded it with a spoon, heated it over the stove, poured melted wax on it, but nothing worked; the polish was just too old. It was not given enough use, his father said; still, he did not put the can back in the box; he left it on the windowsill and it stayed there until someone threw it out.

His father was a nice man; he had a short temper and liked his liquor, true, but he had never done anything to hurt his mother; he had never flown at his mother in a rage, although he often flew into rages and would pound the wall with his fist. He had an awful temper, it was true, but he did not blame his father for this. He must have had a reason. His mother told him he had had a hard family life, his dad, but she wasn't able to describe things in any detail and he was afraid to ask questions because questions made her very nervous. But she could be very nice sometimes, his mother, when she would help him build tents under the kitchen table with a sheet, or let him play store with the tins. When she was like that, he would feel very excited and they would never play for very long; she would always make him go upstairs and calm down, and when he got back, she would be in a very different frame of mind, sitting as she did in the front room or on the porch, sighing and saying her prayers. His father hated the sighing, so she only sighed on weekdays with only him around to hear, and sometimes Eileen, who seemed to be deaf and blind to everything and everybody, as his mother would say, except to her father, whom she adored.

His mother was almost forty-two when she had him, and his father thirty-nine. He didn't notice they were older than his school pals' parents because he never looked at their parents. He didn't like to go into other people's houses; he didn't even like so much to go the cousins' house; he liked staying home and playing on the sidewalk or going down to Abe's for penny candy and baseball cards, but he didn't like going into strange houses. His sister did. She went everywhere. In fact, when she was a teenager, his father and Eileen went to a lot of places together because his mother was ailing, as Eileen put it. The father and daughter would set off of a Sunday morning when it was already hot and the water flat and white, sometimes with the cousins, sometimes not; sometimes on foot, sometimes in the machine; they would pick up a dozen cupcakes somewhere and go over to Uncle

Bill's down the road, or up to Aunt Mary's, just to sit around and pass the time of day, watching the water, setting up the croquet set, having a highball or two; a few times they had driven all the way back to the city to call on Miss Hennessy and her old mother who lived on the parkway; once they had even brought the Hennessys back with them, but that was a mistake, they found, because his mother got all tired out and after dinner had an attack. They were quite the gallivanters, his mother would say, when the two had set off and she and he would play a quick hand of pinochle before it got too hot to move. The ham would be boiling in the Dutch oven for Sunday dinner at two o'clock. What they do, his mother told him time and again, is go out and fill up on sweets, then come home and can't eat their good dinner. But she didn't sound that mad about it; she sounded amused, as if she were talking about children. She never said that to them, when they came home, hot and irritable and full of it; she always sulked and his father sulked, or they had words with each other; once she had thrown a pan of boiling water at him, and he had tried to punch her. Dinner, though, was always quiet, except for the buzzing of flies and mosquitoes, crickets and power lines, motorboats, dry grass and once in a while, the sound of laughing from next door. But the heat was enough to kill you and nobody ate much. He remembered Eileen's white face with the sweat on her upper lip and the wet patches under her arms. His father often ate in shirt sleeves with his collar unfastened; he himself wore a sailor suit or summer shorts and a jacket. His mother put on her best pink crepe dress with the knife-pleated collar and the room smelled of lily of the valley cologne and the salty ham, and the mud and seaweed, if it was low tide. Always at the end of dinner, there'd be a little breeze at the window and all of a sudden you could see gulls up there in the orange of the sky, because it would already be turning orange and a little cooler; someone always would say how another beautiful summer day was passing by. And they would say grace after meals and his mother would move out to the porch to watch the sailboats and read the Sunday rotogravure magazine, while Eileen and he did the dishes. Somedays it was like a picture.

———

That's the way he remembered it, when they still had the house, but the house was long gone. He could see the front stoop out there; it still looked like a front stoop, although lately it seemed like the tides had changed again and it was even farther out and under a few more inches of water. It was a cold day, about thirty degrees, cold even in the sun; the water was a steel blue. There were no boats, no birds, and all the summer houses that were still standing were boarded up. He was looking at the ground, not at the water or the houses—but at a caster wheel on the ground. The funny thing was, he thought, they had never owned anything on wheels that he could remember. He squatted down there on a clean spot, far away from where he thought the house had stood—there were still some marks, or at least he thought he saw marks—and played with the caster. He used to think his mother was a saint, but his wife said once that he only thought it because she had died while he was young and that he was never old enough to understand her. He didn't think one way or the other anymore. His father was still around; he stayed summers in the city with his cronies. He never really thought she was a saint; she had never acted like a saint.

The house was gone now some thirty-five, forty years. It was gone, but there was the stoop. The cousins' house was gone and nothing left of it. All they had of both houses now was the stoop. He had eyes just like his mother's, set deep in his head and settling even deeper with the years. But looking there now at the stoop, his face looked not a bit like his mother's; it lost that sick, sad look; his eyes were blank and filled with the blue of the water.

They Meet a Boy

April could tell Margery was getting boy crazy. She had seen her a few times at the grill, but that was nothing. The next year, she went around with Ellen McGovern, whose brother was expelled from parochial and whose older sister carried a big pocketbook and acted tough. "It'd turn your stomach," April had heard Frances Dooley say when she ran into Ellen at the five and ten—"Hello there, how's your mother?" Mrs. Dooley wore her glasses hanging on a chain around her neck and now her daughter Agnes did. April saw Agnes, two years older but acted a hundred, over in greeting cards, pretending to be looking at cards. Mrs. Dooley wore old lady shoes. She had gone to school with April's father and he was always saying how much he looked up to that woman and the lovely family she had. Mr. Dooley was dead now four years of a heart attack. "She never needed him anyway; she runs that crew," April's mother said. "I wouldn't be so critical (April's father) if I were you." (This came from the front room where everybody thought he was asleep in his chair.) "I think your father's afraid of her," she said to April; "you'd think they were God," she said to him. "You'd be lucky," he said from the front room, "to be doing as good as her with no husband working." "Listen to him," her mother said to April; "if you think she's so great, why don't you go live with them? She'd have you mental in a week."

April's mother was critical of Mrs. Dooley. Even though her brother, Father Joseph Feeney, S.J., sent the family real Hummel figurines from his trips in Germany and she had them out where everybody could see them, plus when he was home she had him over every Sunday with his Mercedes Benz parked right in front where everybody could see it—your father was almost beside himself (April's mother) when he got a load of that—plus the family made such a show of going down to Mass and communion on Sunday all together—just so people can see (ditto) what a lovely family they are—Mrs. Dooley kept a slovenly house and that outweighed everything else. "Typical Irish," April's mother said.

It was April who told her about the slovenly house, in the days she was friends with the younger daughter, Sally, and went over there Saturdays. Mrs. Dooley was always correcting her. "Now Agnes Mary," she said, always calling them by their first and second names, when they didn't have enough personality (April's mother) for one name, "I think they say en-velope these days, don't they? On-velope is passé, April."

"She teaches third grade," April's mother said when she heard it, "she thinks she knows everything."

April's mother could be as nice as pie, as their father would say, if she wanted to be, and Mrs. Dooley, as far as April knew, thought her mother was. She didn't know she was being "belittled" all the time. Mrs. Dooley wasn't that nice either; April had heard her screaming at the kids, and they were model children ("Do you see how nice they speak to people?"), her father said. There was talk she had driven the husband to death with her tongue and that big-shot brother always off to Ireland. "That's what I've heard," her mother said. "I don't know anything about that," her father said, "and you know less."

April was just about to tell Mrs. Dooley her mother was fine, but Mrs. Dooley was looking through the button display to see Ellen McGovern in make-up. Agnes Dooley moved over to buttons too. Mrs. Dooley and April's father had gone to school with Ellen's mother, May Dugan, her name was then; and even then (April's father) people always had something to say about that family. Ellen opened her pocketbook for a bobby pin; she put the pocketbook between her knees and used the bobby pin to hold one side of her hair behind her ear; the other side she fluffed out so the tease would spread a little, but her hair was too skimpy to hold it, April saw, and it just lay flat with a snarl puffed out over the ear. The nuns said it was a disgrace; April thought the Italian girls got theirs to go better—some could get it to stick out half a foot and still be smooth on the outside. Ellen took a big round mirror out and looked at both sides. There was a clink when she closed up the pocketbook and that would be, April figured, the can of hairspray or maybe the chain of Juicy Fruit wrappers they were all making. Ellen had everything they had; she even had the little black ankle boots. They were selling them at the mill now, flat with a pointed toe; skimpy-looking, her mother said; Margery said they were tough-looking.

Ellen McGovern was the only Irish kid in with that kind. Margery despised them. They had a mouth on them, they smoked in the girls' room, they never washed their hair, they'd beat you up right on your own sidewalk if they felt like it, they petted, they hung around after supper in front of Tommy's Pizza and never knew when to go home. The mothers, April knew, would march you straight down to the rectory if they caught you with the white lipstick or the hair; get the tease yanked right out, get the beating of your life. Ellen McGovern put on make-up on the way to school and back-combed her hair in the schoolyard; the nuns would have sent her home to a slap in the mouth if they thought there was anyone there to give it to her.

Mrs. Dooley was going to make a remark. "It makes me sad to see them doing this to themselves, nice girls they are, nice families, and look at them, so cheap-looking. What I don't understand is how the mothers can let them out of the house looking like that." Mrs. Dooley was acting as if she were talking to Agnes, but April knew who she was talking to. "*You're* young," she said, "do you understand it? What do they have to do, the parents, that's so important they can't supervise their own kids?

"Your mother, I know, would never let you out in a rig like that, would she?"

April shrugged. She knew Mrs. Dooley wouldn't go for that, and she didn't. She pushed Agnes right out of the store and didn't even say goodbye. She *did* say that she and Agnes had to be running along to start supper, but April knew those kids didn't have to help—it was just a story—they all had their own rooms and went up there and closed the doors and let her scream bloody murder for all they cared.

April wondered if Ellen were going to get some of her friends to gang up on her because of Mrs. Dooley. She thought about hiding in the back of the store over with the hoses, but it was too late; she knew Ellen had seen her already.

————

These days Margery left her bedroom door unlocked, but she was more stuck up than ever. She started saying the sarcastic things their mother said; she even had a few more pimples on her chin. "Don't look at my face," she was always saying. But if April didn't look at her face, and wasn't supposed to gawk at any of the things in her room, where was she supposed to look? "Oh, don't be such a clown," Margery said when she'd answer the door and see April with her eyes shut. April would have given her a punch to send her into next Tuesday but she no sooner lifted a hand when Margery started yelling and their mother screaming at the foot of the stairs that if they kept up the goddamned bickering, they'd both get a beating they'd never forget when their father got home.

April didn't think they knew Margery was spending so much time with Ellen McGovern, and most of it looking for boys. Their father looked down his nose, as their mother said, at the McGoverns. He didn't even call them McGoverns, he called them by the mother's maiden name, Dugan. The Dugans. May Dugan's father was a drinker and didn't even try to hide it, not that he could have; you'd see him, their father said, in broad daylight coming out of the Old Timers' Tap "stinking." The kids had to raise themselves, they worked after school to keep that family going. The mother, he said, was no better; the whole family would have gone to hell if the old man hadn't drunk himself to death and Mothers' Aid got on her tail, hounded her until she went on the wagon. With him dead, things went okay until the oldest son, Henry Jr., started to run wild and lost his job; he was killed in the war and she was never the same after that, plus ailing with a bum liver; and the two girls, one of them wanted to go into the convent but was refused and you can't blame *them* for that—they have to live with each other day in day out and all under one roof, her father would say when he got started. The Dugan girl, May—the other daughter—finally married, but Jim McGovern was no bargain either. Gambled, plus, the father said, lowering his voice, although April could hear perfectly well from where she was standing, beats her up. Well *I* think, April's mother said, those kids deserve a lot of credit then; they're nice kids in spite of it.

She always stuck up for the McGoverns, even when the boy got expelled. You should get down on your knees and thank God, she said to April, you have a mother and father to take care of you. *He* was the one who would hit the roof when he heard about his kid (April could almost hear him) on the street with the little McGovern like a couple of tramps.

Margery and Ellen were going up to the Cottage Creamery Saturdays after they ironed their bermudas and tried to get out of the house in just loafers and no socks, but Margery's mother—although she didn't know where they were going—put a stop to that the first time she came home on a hot afternoon, late for confession and her feet all orange, the new loafers stretched out, and supposed to last another school year. Margery nearly got cracked for that, but she had them off in a minute and covered the orange feet with black knee socks and a pair of oxfords she always refused to wear.

That wasn't the only problem. Saturday the house got cleaned and their mother didn't feel she could spare them until the last Venetian blind slat was dusted and all the rooms smelling of ammonia, every window in the house flung open. Margery and Ellen made plans to go at 1:30, early enough so they could take their time and go past St. John Chrysostom's, all boys; but the work wasn't usually done until 3:00 or 3:30 if everyone decided to take a little rest after lunch in the kitchen, where all the "clutter" from the rest of the house: unemptied wastebaskets, dust rags, bottles, breakfast dishes accumulated; plus the washing machine going, the cellar door and cupboard doors open, a mess. One-thirty was a hard time to try and get out of it. Their mother didn't want to hear complaints or sighing either. "It's not my dirt; *I* didn't do this," she would say. She was always telling them how they made her job harder, she had to be pushing them all the time, when if they would only do it willingly, they could all be done and relax.

It was hard getting started in the morning, blinds and shades all shut from the night before and the house "smelling like a den." She would hustle them both upstairs; too many times, she said, she had caught them with their nose in a magazine if she left them downstairs alone to work. Margery sighed right up to the end, when their mother would put pin curls in the hair she had washed in the morning, tie a scarf around them and take a little nap on the couch with a baby blanket around her shoulders, "Okay, go out; you can all go out now. Don't be hanging around here pestering me." They would go out, but they had to be back by quarter of five to go down to church for confession and after that, supper and maybe a half hour free after supper and that was it: bath, TV programs, bed.

––––––––––

It was in the schoolyard Margery had found out about the Creamery. Ellen was folding gum wrappers. Margery fished a few singles out of her own pocketbook. You didn't have to buy anything, Ellen explained, the boys stood in front of the picture window, or on the wall of the old Ursuline school.

Margery thought Ellen was making it up. She was always telling stories, ever since grade one. Then she had told them the bishop came to her house every Thursday and ate a hotdog, and that her father's father was the bishop's father's cousin. She told them she had a sister in college out of state, her mother and father were born in Ireland—Margery's father laughed when he heard that one, said Eddie Dugan was born right over Silverman's Market, if she thought that was Ireland—that her mother gave her a five-dollar bill every Saturday and let her go downtown on the bus and buy anything. Then someone saw Ellen one Saturday morning playing with the Flynn kids in the churchyard until the priest came out and chased them away.

But Margery believed her this time because she hadn't lied in ages. She didn't say anything anymore. The nuns were always trying to get her to speak up, but every time she did, her face would turn red and they'd have to send her down to the basement for a drink.

"Do *you* talk to them?" Margery asked her. Ellen said you didn't have to talk. Margery couldn't picture it. Later, when Mother Agatha was reading them out of the European history book and every page sounded alike, she figured Ellen might be making it up just to get someone to go with her. Ellen was more popular when she was lying. The kids followed her around in the schoolyard in a big pack.

The nuns had put a good scare into her, though, when one of her stories got to them—it might have been the one about the bishop

51

eating hotdogs on Thursday; more likely it was the one that got them out asking Mrs. McGovern for a favor based on what Ellen said about the $5 a week allowance, then embarassed to find that Mr. McGovern was out of work and the family was making do on $52 a week unemployment.

At first, there was going to be an immediate suspension, but they kept her in school instead and made her stay for detention every night for a month. She had to sit at her desk "lips sealed" until quarter of four when she went to all the classrooms and emptied the wastebaskets into the brazier in the schoolyard. Everybody knew she was scared stiff of fire and cried the whole time. The janitor sat on the schoolyard steps and smoked a cigarette, just sat and watched until Ellen was done. Then he put the baskets back and put the fire out. Ellen McGovern ran all the way home—April had seen her tearing by a little before five when she was getting ready to turn on "Leave It to Beaver."

Ellen stayed after every night for two weeks until the nun in the homeroom got lenient and made her do it every other day because the baskets weren't that full. Her mother came up to school the last part of the second week and told them she needed Ellen home nights to take care of the younger ones while she did the marketing.

The nun—after saying that never in all her years of teaching had she seen a child who always had a lie on her lips—excused her from the remainder of the punishment. She warned Mrs. McGovern to keep a close eye as she got into the teenage years because that one, she said, pointing at the empty desks, was looking for trouble.

When Ellen had brought the first note home, she was given a good slap and a beating when her father got home and all worked up about it. No play after school and the girl could get up an hour early weekdays and get herself down to morning Mass so they could see someone was doing their duty by the child. They were there at the seven, all the nuns; the whole community saw little Ellen McGovern, who was told to sit in the front row and act like a lady. She went up to communion first when everyone knew to wait for the nuns to go first. The homeroom nun was glad to see the child down on her knees. She wasn't a bad girl—they all knew that—but bad companions, not the right kind of training at home (although they themselves had taught the mother; but the Dugans, everybody knew,

52

were not the average family). Maybe, since they had caught it in time, they could set her on the right path, the grade one nun told the principal, who thought too much had been made of her fibs, but told Mother Anna "God willing," and left it at that. The principal had been staying after school, too, to make sure little Ellen didn't get locked in the classroom. The girl was asked to stop in at the office before going home and the principal sometimes gave her a hard candy from the box in the supply closet. "Run along, Dearie," she always said, getting her own cloak and overshoes out, "Don't dillydally now."

Half of the principal's nightly recreation was taken up waiting for Ellen McGovern to finish her detention. She was anxious to get home for the last half hour and chat with her friend, Mother Dorothy, who taught English and music to the upper grades and had heard the story of Ellen McGovern from start to finish and found it funny. She spoke to the child whenever she saw her, partly because none of the lower-grade nuns and few of the children did, since she had been in disgrace. All her responsibilities in homeroom were taken away: putting the new chalk out and opening the upper windows with the pole. She was not called on to take a message or pass out the straws for milk. She was hardly ever called on for an answer, and when she was, they called her "Miss" and all the girls turned around in their seats to look. The trouble was going to be "entered (the nuns) into her permanent record" for high school teachers, employers, anyone who wanted, to see. It would follow her, they said, everywhere she went in life. This is what could happen if children were deceitful. In the second grade, two little boys cried and the nun didn't mention the permanent record again. In the seventh grade—and the seventh grade nun should have known better because she had taught seventh for years and knew what they were like, but she was told to say it and she said it—they made fun of it. Mother Agatha could hardly calm them down afterwards: rolling pencils up their ties, slamming the desk tops down, making popping noises with their mouths. Mother Agatha told the worst one (one she had complete control over: she was always bragging about this to the other nuns) to open a window and take a deep breath, all of them, and when Eddie Curran got up to do it, the others quieted down and the matter was never discussed again. Someone pointed Ellen McGovern out to Mother Agatha one day, but her eyesight wasn't good; she remembered the older brother, though, the one who was expelled, a hooligan. "I had him in detention four nights out of five," she said, "but come Christmas, there he was at the convent door ready to help out with the Christmas baskets." She was surprised, hearing the story, that Ellen McGovern was such a *little* girl, but glad she didn't have to teach them at that age, little ninnies they were.

———

Sick of having to look at that long face, and they were almost done anyway: "Go, go if you have to," Margery's mother said that Saturday. Down in the kitchen, a second load of wash was thrown in, and reheating the breakfast coffee; "So where are you in such a hurry to get to?"

"Out," Margery in her pink and purple madras shorts.

There would have been a discussion but for April climbing up the cellar stairs with a transparent plastic Visible Woman doll, red and blue rubber veins. "Where are you going with that toy?" "It isn't a toy." April had gotten the doll two Christmases ago, and it still didn't work. "If *you* think," Margery heard, racing down the porch steps, "we're done now, just because that one got out of it, you've got another think—." Margery cut through the backyard past the kitchen windows; they hadn't even finished cleaning up one mess, she heard her mother say, when April was all set to start another. "I have news for you, my girl."

After all the hurrying, Ellen wasn't ready. Margery called her from outside the back door, no answer, knocked on the window. Ellen's baby brother, Henry, came to the door with a plastic gun and pointed it. "Is Ellen home, Henry?" The little boy turned around and "Ellie, belly," yelled, "the girl's here." He had tomato on his mouth and some of the front of his shirt. Margery moved around him and walked into the back hall, boots and rubbers, schoolbags, milk bottles, clothespins all over the floor, to the kitchen. No one in the kitchen but Henry. "Just a sec, tell her just a sec," Margery heard. Henry held out his fingers, "one, two second, three," and ran out of the kitchen. He came back and looked in the doorway; "What's your name?" Margery sat down on the only kitchen chair without a pile of laundry on it. He said it again and ran out of the room. Margery heard

someone on the steps. "Ma," shrieked, "there's a girlie down here."
In the doorway again with a silly grin. "My mumma said to—" and
right behind him, pushing him a little into the broom closet, Ellen.
"Get out of my way." "Ma, she hit me." "Shut up." She picked him
up before he got his mouth open again and plunked him down on a
pile of diapers. "Hold on," seeing him rock back and forth, "or you'll
crack your skull." They watched him a minute. "I'll be ready one
second, Marge." Ellen put the kettle on the burner and picked up one
of the wood matches scattered over the top of the stove.

"Didn't you eat yet?"

"Yes, stupid, see," pulling a wrinkled pink ribbon out of her shirt
pocket. When the steam came out, she ran the ribbon across the
spout until it dangled smooth and limp. "I'm almost ready," she said,
out of the kitchen. "Ma, your water's boiling." It was already two and
they hadn't even gotten out of the house.

Henry slipped off the diapers and lay his head on them, with an eye
on the girl. When Margery looked, he buried his face. Screamed
when he saw she was still looking at him, ran out of the room, hid
behind the closet door, peekaboo. Margery looked at the clock. It
was on the wall between two windows, fingermarks all over the
bottom of the windows, on the woodwork, the yellow walls. They left
the cereal boxes out on the table, crumbs all around the toaster and
someone had knocked the salt shaker over. Under the table was a big
red truck. Margery couldn't see the pantry from where she was, but
she knew it was full of dirty dishes. They didn't even use real dish
detergent; Margery had seen Ellen throw in a cake of Ivory to float in
the gray water.

She heard someone on the stairs, but it was too heavy and slow.
"Hello, Mrs. McGovern," she said, before the woman even reached
the hallway door. "Who's that I hear? Well look who it is. Don't you
look nice." Mrs. McGovern fixed a cup of tea and moved the diapers
to the high chair to sit opposite and visit. Henry ran in and hid
behind his mother. "Come out, you little silly," she said, trying to
drag him out from behind. "Well, stay there then and be a baby." "I
am *not* a baby." "Well, come out of there behind your mother and act
like a man. Go upstairs and tell Miss that Margery is getting sick and
tired of cooling her heels while she primps in front of that mirror."

"So, how are things with the Flanaghan family?" the lady said, putting three sugars, yellow and lumpy, into her tea. She was wearing Sunday clothes, navy blue crepe dress and stockings. Margery didn't see how she could do housework dressed in her gladrags. She had a few pin curls and a hairnet over the gray hair, black circles under her eyes, chapped lips. Maybe they were going to a wedding. "Son," she said, after a few minutes of just sitting there, "run upstairs and tell that girl to get herself down here."

Mrs. McGovern was looking at something. Margery turned around and wondered if it was the calendar or just the wall. "It's the fourteenth," she said, "What?" "How are you?" "Oh fine, thank you dear, and yourself?" Now she was staring at the door. "Well," she said suddenly, picking up her cup of tea and reaching for a pack of Viceroys on the back of the stove, "I'm going to sit here a minute now and collect my thoughts. You girls have a nice time." She walked out of the kitchen, Henry right behind her. "Come on, my boy." Margery heard her settling into a chair and rocking. "Hi Ma, bye Ma." That was Ellen. She had tied the ribbon around her head and let the ends hang down her back; it wasn't a ribbon after all, Margery noticed, it was the sash from a dress. She had put orange lipstick on. "It's on crooked (Margery, as soon as they were outside), wipe some off." "I can't see to do it, you do it." They stopped in the middle of the sidewalk and Margery took a tissue from her pocketbook and dabbed at Ellen's mouth; she still looked like she had just eaten a popsickle. "That's the best I can do. Just keep wetting your lips. See if you can bite some of it off." "Thanks, you're a big help." And there was her mother right in the window watching. "Your mother's spying," Margery said. "Hurry up or she'll drag me back in."

———

But it was all a waste, Margery must have said a million times on the way home an hour and a half later. Don't blame it on me, Ellen said, you're the one that chickened out. The orange lips had faded after two ice waters and a lime freeze. Besides, this was just the first time, she added; don't be such a stick.

A block away from the McGovern house, Margery felt better. She stopped to look at the coming attractions at the Palace, making sure Ellen was not going to spring around the corner and pester her some more. "Gidget Goes Hawaiian" was coming. It had been coming a long time, but "Butterfield Eight," For Adults (the Legion of Decency) with Reservations, was still playing. Gidget was standing in front of a palm tree in a two-piece bathing suit. Her hair was tied back in a ponytail and there was a boy behind the tree with a lei around his neck, James Darren—peeyu, the other Gidget boyfriends were better. The tree was next to a skyscraper hotel and Margery thought she could make out Gidget's mother standing on one of the porches gawking. Maybe it was the chaperone. He was cute, even if it was James Darren, 29, married with a baby. The movie magazines said he wanted to divorce his wife, but he didn't look that old in the picture in his bathing suit, sneaking up on her. There were some cute boys at the Creamery, standing up against the wall. Margery and Ellen had to squeeze past them to get two seats next to each other on the counter, but no one had paid any attention. They couldn't even get waited on it was so crowded, and then when they did, Margery had to spend most of her allowance so they could keep their place and not be thrown out. Ellen hadn't said there'd be so many girls there from the high school with loafers and shoulder bags, drinking coffee. The boys stood right behind *them* and they kept swiveling around in their seats.

Margery was acting so nervous, Ellen had to tell her not to have a conniption. No one ever came near them except stupid Arthur Ready, who used to live next door to them in the old house and had gone into the army, but came right out with flat feet. He was a jerk, everyone knew he was a jerk, plus the last thing Margery had heard was he was going away next year to be a Christian Brother. "So why doesn't he go?" Ellen said to Margery after he had gone to get his half gallon of ice cream.

He had asked about the family and if Margery had heard the news from the old neighborhood. Margery said she hadn't. "Well, you know Jimmy Burke who used to live on the corner across from the McElroys? My mother told me she heard he almost got a girl in trouble down the beach." "Really?" Ellen said, and she didn't even *know* the Burkes. Margery didn't know whether she remembered him or not. "Was he the guy Jackie Toohey used to push around in that old baby carriage?" "That was *me*. Jimmy was the one used to steal the apples from Crazy Annie, remember?" Margery didn't remember— April was the one who was friendly with Crazy Annie and used to take her up the rotten apples that she put in her oven. "Give my best to your folks, and make sure you tell your mother."

"He thinks he's so smart," Margery told Ellen when he finally left. "My mother told me when I was little not to pay any attention to him—a little tapioca," she said, tapping her forehead. "He's not that bad," Ellen said.

Then Ellen told her to mind her seat a minute while she went to the ladies' room and that's when it all happened. Margery laid a napkin down on Ellen's stool. She wanted to look at where Ellen had gone but there were all those boys. She looked quick and saw the long line in front of the ladies' room, Ellen at the end of it. She watched the waiters for a while to take her mind off it. A tall boy in glasses was making a strawberry cabinet with vanilla ice cream for an old lady who wanted two small cups to drink it in.

The lady was pouring herself a second glassful of pink stuff and wiping her lips with a hankie when Margery, taking quick looks in that direction, saw Ellen come out of the bathroom and walk through the crowd waiting in line to buy an ice cream cone, and that other line against the wall. She stopped right in front of the first boy, white shirt and dungarees with short brown hair combed down on his forehead—Margery had seen him coming in—the cutest one, she couldn't believe her eyes. The old lady with the strawberry cabinet turned around to make a face at Ellen. "Move along, dearie," Margery could hear her as plain as day, and so could everyone else, "don't loiter there right behind me." Ellen flattened herself out against the wall, but there wasn't any wall left so she had to move in front of the door and get out of the way every minute so people could pass. "So bold they are," the lady said to the customer on her left, a high school girl eating a hotdog, who stared at her, then turned to get a look at Ellen and give her a look, then back to whisper something to her girlfriend.

Finally Ellen moved down the aisle and sat down next to Margery. People were still looking and Margery was right up on her feet. "Where're you going?" but Margery was off the stool and toward the side door. The old lady was pointing them out with her spoon; Margery could have slapped that stupid Ellen right in the face, and never talk to her again, but there was something she wanted to get straight first.

"So what did *you* have to talk to him about, if you don't mind my asking?"

She had just asked him, Ellen said, if he were at the high school now and if he knew a kid called Eddie McAloon.

"You made that up," Margery screamed, then covered her mouth because they were walking on the sidewalk in front of the old convent.

"So what?"

"What'd he say?"

"He asked me if this Eddie McAloon played basketball. I said I thought so."

Margery screamed again. Ellen started laughing and got Margery laughing and they laughed all the way down School Street. The Eddie McAloon they knew, the one who lived over Bell's, was two years old.

I think they would have talked to us, Ellen said, if it wasn't for that old biddy. She kept telling me—get this—that I was in her light. Ellen was trying to get Margery laughing again, but Margery didn't want to laugh. Ellen was hoping she would just forget about being mad, but she didn't feel like it yet. A whole day was wasted and now they had to wait another week. "You had fun, admit it," Ellen said, before turning into the house. "Just drop it, would you mind," Margery said, but by the time she was up the hill and almost home, she thought it might have been the best time she had ever had, going over it and how close they had come. It had almost happened—they had missed it by a hair.

Providence, 1970:
Behind This Soft Eclipse

She is sitting at the kitchen table in front of a pile of nickels, waiting to play skat with her grandnephew. She hung her black lambswool coat in the cold front closet next to a blue raincoat and a fur stole, and ran her hand along the satin lining, fingering the embroidered patch over the inside pocket. There used to be a hanky in there with L initialed in silk thread, lily of the valley scent. There is a plastic tube somewhere, too, criss-cross and a startling feeling of lightness in her shoes as if they were still stuffed with paper. The cold is still, satiny. The front hallway has three doors, two leading in, one out: do they make them like that anymore? No.

The grandnephew is eating peanuts. He has loosened his black knit tie and unbuttoned the top button of his shirt. He is reading an article spread over the top of an ad for rubber hoses and garden furniture, and has covered some of her nickels with the newspaper. She gathers up the nickels, drops them one by one into an old coffee jar. He is sitting in her place across from the sink. His mother used to fix her a whiskey and water in a tall glass with a pheasant on it. She had a pile of nickels and a pile of peanuts, but he always won. There were other people at the table too, a gray and white chrome kitchen table with a smooth, easy surface for cards, but he always won.

He didn't see the peanut that had fallen into the fold of the newspaper and he put his elbow on it. He brushed the peanut skins off his suit jacket without losing his place. She could see it was something about water; he had always liked water sports. He read the very last line, then reread the first paragraph; she smiled; he turned the page and there was one of the nickels. He looked at it, scanned the page for something new to read, reached into the bowl for nuts. She leaned over to read his face, knowing that if *he* had left something, she would have found it. He decided to skip that article and turned the pages to the end of the section and read what was on the back.

His mother used to remove the table cover and turn the overhead light on. He would turn down the TV and she would push herself out of the old green armchair with both freckled fists. They could hear her coming, the strong leg and the lame leg.

She was good at cards and would have won if he hadn't always played. She still had her own teeth and she could eat whatever he ate, even Brazil nuts, but she had a hard time sitting on those metal kitchen chairs. She told him time and again that it was these particular ones; she could, for instance, sit on her own kitchen chairs, which were wood and had no padding at all, for hours on end. It was the structure that counted.

He must be looking for something: he flipped from section to section, back-paging, wetting his finger—which she could see already had ink on it. He was thin and his white shirt sank in a little at the chest; his shoulders were like padded hangers. That's what she had left his mother, padded hangers—the ones she had been hoarding since she was first married, and which his mother had always admired, although she never bought any for herself. (There wasn't a single padded hanger in their front closet—only wire ones.) She wondered if his mother would use them; perhaps she would keep them all for her own closet, although there were certainly plenty to go around. She had tied them in bunches with ribbons and had written his mother's name on a cardboard tag, printing "all of them" under the name. After all those years of collecting, she had amassed enough of the satin brocaded kind to hang all her nightgowns. His mother had already sold the dining room furniture and the kitchen set and the ladder-back chairs from the living room; perhaps, she might have kept them for him, but that was their business. They had their own ideas; he had his own ideas even though he was the image of her sister, not quite as frail.

He had liked beating her at cards. She wasn't the kind of old person you had to cater to. She understood jokes and told a few herself, her crooked hands curled around a pack of cigarettes at the edge of the table. She was catty and said whatever she thought, which led people to believe she might have a little something tucked away. But if she had, surely he might have come into a little. It was all gone; it had been eaten up; it must have been sunk in that business of her husband's, and him dead so many years. None of them—not his brother, not him, not hers—had any business sense. She could still shake her head, although it felt thick, crammed with thoughts and was it all to remain as it was now, unchanged? But he looked ready to play. He was brushing peanut skins off his pants and tidying the sections of paper.

He put the nickel in his pocket and prepared to deal the cards: a green pack with scenes of the seasons on the backs. The one with the bent corner—everybody knew this—was the three of spades. The cards clicked as he shuffled them. She opened her purse to get her plastic cuffs and drew them on, stuffing Kleenex under the wristbands. A card sailed across the table to her hands. She thought it might be a jack. He reached out and turned it over; it was the five of hearts. He flipped it back again and continued the deal.

———

She had lain in her bed, a white painted bed with an orange wool blanket, for nearly six months. The years stuck together, lying there, in uneven packs, with always the same side face up—the blue glass ball and the tin tub of bubbles were all there was of childhood; Ethel and Nellie in those white lace dresses with straw hats, standing in front of the pier (she could hardly see their faces for the glare), and the old man (that was him) bent over the black enamel table with a jeweler's glass in his eye (he also wore a hearing aid); the curly dog who lay on the braided rug; the pan of penuche and the long-handled spoon; and every lovely Thanksgiving Day for the last ten years with a bowl of grapes and nuts, a rubber band around the cards, the orange glare from the overhead light and her pink slippers side by side under the table. She also used the cuffs to write letters—the script was billowy, with a small erratic tremor—and there were splats of ink. There was ink on the cuffs, plastic cuffs, double thick with a molasses-like stain between the layers.

He turned one card over, and placed it right-side up next to the deck and gathered up his own hand, rearranging suits and values. She tried to pick up her hand, but it was like gathering soot—her fingers were the wrong thickness and besides, she knew he wanted to play her hand too. He gathered up her cards and arranged them face up on the table. She smiled to think he'd be capable of playing their hands, both hands, without cheating. He lit a cigarette and laid it on the edge of the table.

She won a game. He had let her win. Her hand was good, true, but she never would have played it the way he played it, holding back till the end. Hooray, she yelled, when she saw the queen and jack triumph suddenly, one-two. He would have had to coordinate her hand against his hand to do it. She never would have played it that way. She couldn't have feigned the absence of value and held the strong color cards till the end. But he had laid up her cards against his, and over his. She had won. She opened the nickel jar, but it was too heavy to lift out of her drawstring purse and besides, it was late and time for him to be driving her home. So she stripped off her cuffs and folded them one into the other, and he dumped the rest of the peanuts back into the jar. She hoped that, when she was gone, he would make himself a nice turkey sandwich or something. She went for her coat, leaning against the lining, cool as water; the light in the kitchen, where he was, was like a tent. Outside that one door was air. That had never been his element. It would be hers pretty soon now, and a chilly ride of a Sunday into the country.

The Hospital:
Seeing Him There Almost Dead

They only got up to the Creamery one more time that summer. School started and Margery (even Ellen McGovern was going to St. Mary's Academy—and Mr. Flanaghan didn't see how "that one" could afford it) was going to public. She went up her first day all alone, but she was glad to go, glad to have somewhere to go and be out of the way for a while. The night before, when she was picking out an outfit to wear the first day and April was sitting on the bed helping, but no help at all because she liked everything, April said it was everyone's worst summer and wouldn't it be nice getting back to school with Christmas coming. So what else is new? Margery said, you love school. You know what I mean, April said, crossing her legs, trying to find the loafer she had dropped.

Their father had been rushed to the hospital with a bleeding ulcer June 4th and hadn't come out for good till the middle of August. He had almost died—once from bleeding that no one knew about, and then again after the second operation. They were up to visit him every day. Now he was home again, but not much better and the doctors still didn't know what was causing the trouble, there were so many things wrong and they had taken out everything they could take out.

All June and July they sat in the air-conditioned lobby with the green linoleum and the white statue of Our Lady of Lourdes, the Dominican nun at the reception desk giving out news over the phone—"No one's up there now, I'm sorry," was one of the ways she put it when someone had died; they figured that out right away. The

"Mr. Green is not with us anymore," was even easier. They had to wait in the lobby during the operations and then while he was in the intensive care ward. Twice when April had visited the first day—and they only had three visits, each spread out over the whole day—he was asleep and she stood there by the bed—more like a crib than a bed, with the high sides—until her legs got tired, then sat on a metal chair in front of the nurses' station and looked into her father's corner. At least ten people in the ward, but she knew his snoring. Every time one of the nurses moved away from one of the TV monitors behind the desk, April—who was twelve and knew you had to be fifteen or they'd throw you out—jumped up and went to stand by the bed again. He wasn't snoring at all; you could hardly tell he was breathing. He didn't have his false teeth in and his mouth was caved in; otherwise, he looked peaceful, as her mother had said, and not in the terrible pain they had been thinking of.

———

April had never seen her mother in such a good mood for so long a time. They had gotten into a routine and after seven o'clock Mass and communion, they stopped to have a donut and coffee on the way to the hospital, then settled into the same three chairs in the lobby, after asking the nun if there was a change in the word on their father's index card. He wasn't on the danger list anymore; for almost a week he had been "fair." They knew "fair" was bad, but as long as he didn't move backward, fair was on the optimistic side, their mother said.

After she talked to the nun—and she had to go first to ask; she had a fit if they heard before her—their mother came over and sat with them. They had to wait till 9:30 for the first visit; she took out a shopping pad from her pocketbook and they played hangman or tick-tack-toe until April found the Quizzle book in the gift shop and they did test-your-skill puzzles and riddles, which were more interesting. It was fun and sometimes they got a little giddy so early in the morning with the glaring sun coming through the plate glass, making their mother's eyes water and heating the place up. At 9:30 she went upstairs and Margery and April sat with the empty chair between them, Margery saying how tired she was and April saying she was tireder. April sometimes got up to look in the dark gift-shop window, or to go to the bathroom. She put it off as long as she could—the smell of ether made her gag; it wasn't ether, her mother said, it was disinfectant. Margery didn't get up because it was her turn next and she was always quiet—moody, their mother said—before. By the time April went, he wasn't even alert enough to talk to, and he was very eager to talk, they all knew that. "I think it's made him a little tapioca," their mother said, because of how happy he was to be there; "he's thrilled," she kept saying. "He's already made a friend up there; he doesn't give them any trouble at all; they think he's so nice."

Sometimes his eyes would close in the middle of a sentence, and he wouldn't wake up until April was gone. But it was okay, she told them, because he always talked a blue streak in the afternoon. They were always bragging about his talking. He hardly said a word at home. The only one who didn't seem to find it such a novelty was Margery; she hated talking to him.

She hated talking to him at home, but it wasn't as noticeable there. April knew how fast Margery could vanish from a room as soon as her father came into it. The only time she couldn't escape was at the supper table, but Margery didn't talk to anyone at the supper table. She set her chair closer to her mother and angled it away from him. This had all come, April figured, from the time he had told Margery how he never wanted to see her on the street with those squashed heels—he didn't know the name, but they both knew what he meant—he was always seeing on young girls; they look so cheap. April couldn't believe he noticed something like that, because he never noticed anything. But Margery being a teenager now was something he *did* notice, at least Margery thought he did. "I see them out there, girls your age, chasing the boys; it's enough to make you sick!" It made him mad just to think about it. April told Margery she understood; it gave her a peculiar feeling, too, hearing him all of a sudden get so worked up.

"I don't see why you're picking on me, I haven't done anything," Margery would say, then get up and leave the table. There would be an argument about who was at fault, until April got involved and they started on her.

Margery thought her father didn't like teenagers, but she didn't realize, April pointed out, that he *did* like them, he was just afraid she'd turn into a bad one. Margery told April to mind her own business, but April said at least this was something he was interested

66

in, and not to be such a baby. Margery slammed her bedroom door. When April started it up another time, Margery said, "Why are you sticking up for him; you hate his guts." Well, even if she did, you had to pity him, she told Margery, he's had such an awful life. You sound just like her, Margery said.

April tried to be nicer so his feelings wouldn't get hurt. But he was always able to tell when April was, as her mother put it, being a phony. "Don't *you* do me any favors"—and he was even shorter with her. "You're being a martyr for nothing," Margery said.

The harder Margery was on her father, and she was treating him worse and worse—she wouldn't answer even if he asked in a nice way—the easier he seemed to be on her. Even their mother was on Margery's back less often. She got her way all the time, April thought. Plus, the quieter and grouchier Margery got, the more April got in trouble, every night told to leave the table before her father flew into a rage from irritation. Just for talking, she told Margery, he's at me, and I have to talk to somebody, don't I?

Things had gotten about as bad as they could when he got sick, and then they all got some relief. Even though their mother said he had brought it all on himself by how nervous and worked up he could get over nothing, she was not as critical of him while he was in the hospital and especially after the operations. In between times, when they kept him in there to recuperate, he acted just like himself, fretting about nothing, grouchy, moody, no interest in anything, no conversation except about problems that he could get all excited about. It was only, and April noticed it first, when he was very sick that he was normal.

The first operation everyone got through okay; the second was an ordeal. After the first one, there was supposed to be nothing in there that could go wrong, so no one knew what they would find the second time, plus no one was optimistic because the first one had only made him good for a few months. The operation took five hours: five hours the three of them sat in the lobby, from seven o'clock with no reports, nothing, no sign the operation was even going on. The last time, the doctor had sent someone out in the middle—and it was only a two-hour operation—to tell them it was all right, it was almost over, that the ulcer was there and they got it. No one came out this time. They tried to keep their spirits up—and Margery was more of a help than she had ever been in her life, their mother kept saying—but it was hard, the time went by so slow, and there was nothing in any of it to base your hopes on.

At ten o'clock, they waited a few minutes more to see if maybe one of the assistants in a pale green suit with a green hat wouldn't be coming out any second now through the swing door with the porthole with something to say, but no. It was Margery who had the idea of checking with the switchboard operator to find out if Dr. Whiting was still operating, because she would have to know his whereabouts, wouldn't she?

"We don't know, dear," the nun—it wasn't the one they were used to, who was taking a little vacation, she had told them the day before, to the south county house "a stone's throw from the beach," and their mother said she was glad to hear it, it would do her good—said. The replacement, a young one with very thick eyebrows, hadn't time to talk; the phone rang all morning. When she wasn't answering it and flipping through the stack of index cards, April saw her open a little prayerbook. April could see her mother watching too, although the nun was quick to whisk the prayerbook off the desk when someone came in the front door. Under normal circumstances, April knew, her mother would have a remark to make, so *she* made it. "See, praying for her is like goofing off for everybody else." Her mother didn't laugh, but Margery did. "That's what you'd do if you had the job."

After two hours the nun finally unbent, as their mother said later, running through the events of the day with April and Margery when they stopped for a late lunch at the tearoom, a treat. The nun got up from the desk during a lull and with her hands folded asked them if they were waiting for anyone in particular (April couldn't believe she had already forgotten) and if there was anything she could do. Their mother explained again and the nun said she understood and that it was all right for them to stay there in the lobby and wait. Imagine, their mother said, her thinking we would up and leave the place with your father—not knowing if he was dead or alive—just on her say so. But then she only had the heart to be polite, or maybe it was April who was polite, but the nun went back to her desk and sat there smiling at them. She got up again at 9:30 to say she would offer up a prayer for their father's speedy recovery. Everybody was polite. At 10:45 she told them, without getting up, that the cafeteria was open now and she was sure they could use a hot cup of tea and a bite to eat. Their mother said no, they would just sit there in case, but then changed her mind. "I know *you're* hungry," she said to April. "Well, let's go then." "We know where you are," the nun said smiling, "in case."

Wasn't she an odd duck? their mother said in the elevator, and April and Margery took turns remembering the funny little things. "Did you see her lips move?" April started to laugh. "They did!" "And the handkerchief stuck up her sleeve? Imagine blowing your nose in it and putting it back." Her mother gave April a warning look. "That's enough now. . . . What killed me was the way she said the same thing over and over, so stiff. I bet she scares people to death." April started laughing again. They were at the cafeteria doors and her mother told her not to act so silly, to put her shoulders back and be a lady. "What if one of his doctors is down here and he sees you."

The three of them, Margery now taller than her mother, light brown hair, smooth skin ("She's going to be a looker, that one," her mother said just yesterday when Margery got up to go the the bathroom); April, a foot shorter, dark hair, glasses, round shoulders, no waist ("You should watch all the calories you're putting into yourself; you're at the age now," her mother said, when it was a question of pie or cake for dessert); the mother, forty, small, dark-haired, slimmer than April, not as slim as Margery, hugging the strap of her pocketbook to the body. She was ahead of them now, although she had the smallest step and rested all her weight on each one, where Margery had a light, toes-in, stiff-legged walk, and April the least energetic of all, feet barely skimming the floor. Her mother was always telling her not to be so heavy on her feet, but she was actually a quiet walker and you could hardly tell when she was coming.

They had a quick lunch: Margery and her mother, toasted cheese sandwiches and coffee—Are you drinking coffee now? the mother said to Margery, as Margery was spooning in three sugars. "Ma, I have it every day at home." "Oh, I know you drink it in the morning, but you're getting just like me now—have to have it everywhere." "I like it, too," April said, hearing the tone.

"Eat up and let's get back upstairs. You act as if we're on a pleasure trip," looking at April.

69

"Look at her, she's doing it too."

April had a cheeseburger and orangeade. She finished first and kept turning to look at the wall clock. "We've been here ten minutes—that means it's been four hours and twenty, thirty, almost thirty minutes since he's been in." April turned back expecting the usual discussion about what and how long and how much longer, but it didn't start. Her mother and Margery were eating. Her mother ate just the part inside the crusts and piled the crusts and toothpicks in the middle of the plate. "Finish up now, girls."

Things had changed, April was thinking, if those two were ganging up against her; they had never gotten along, never stuck up for each other. Their mother had been saying lately that in times like this families stick together and don't bicker and wrangle all the time, but April was surprised Margery took it so seriously. Before the operation, she hadn't said so much as a sentence to her mother voluntarily; ever since she was a little girl, she didn't talk much. So what had happened? Margery had grown up is what her mother said; now she thought of other people instead of only thinking of herself (like April) all the time. April didn't think it was that. There was something she was trying to hide, and she was being friendly just in case it got out, so she'd be on everybody's good side.

Their mother had been telling them since they were little that it took just a little thought and consideration, a few simple tasks around the house and people would be more than satisfied. Neither of them paid attention to this because the few things were impossible when you had other things to do, but now it seemed to April that Margery was doing them and being a hypocrite. It was a lot of baloney; underneath it all Margery still hated their guts.

The thing that April thought she had to hide was not something in school like before, because she was passing in her business courses— in ninth grade she'd gotten out of everything she couldn't pass, and wasn't causing any trouble that anyone knew about. But she had a boyfriend, Jerry—the parents knew that much—and Jerry, a senior in high, bunked school with Margery on Wednesdays and came back to the house. They got there right after their mother left for her part-time job, clerk typist at the valve plant on East Main. April had come home from school on Wednesday during Corpus Christi devotions because she had forgotten her beanie and the homeroom nun

70

was strict about not letting them put a Kleenex on their head in church. She came in her usual way, across the lawn past the living room windows, and there they were, making out on the couch. April scrunched down in the hedge and peeked through the window; they were still there, right in the house for everyone to see and April kept seeing it. It would kill him if he could see it.

April made a lot of racket on the back porch, kicked the metal box full of empty milk bottles, slammed the door, pounded up and down the steps. By the time she got inside, nobody was home. They must have run out the front, down the sidewalk and around the corner. April couldn't see anyone on the street, or maybe they were hiding somewhere behind the house. She went back in and straightened the couch cover; it was all wrinkled and just think of their poor mother spending her hard-earned pay buying the slipcovers and having this happen to them so soon; they were hardly broken in, plus him sick all the time now, coughing and throwing up all night long; it was too much and April fell flat down on the couch and buried her head, but it came right up again because the couch smelled of a boy. She picked the cushions up and banged them against the arm to air them out.

Never again did she catch them like that, but she knew—Margery must have known too—that they'd be caught sooner or later. For one thing, the school knew they were bunking. How come the principal, April wondered, wasn't always sending them notices home? Just as well he was in the hospital and not home to get the news whenever it might come.

That's why Margery was going out of her way to be nice and act like a grown-up. Their mother was in for a little surprise. Margery, as usual, finished last and they all went into the ladies' room together. It was a big ladies' room, two rooms, one filled with easy chairs and couches for the nurses. While Margery fussed with her hair, her mother sat down and put her feet up. She asked April to get her the paper lying under an ashtray on the end table. She read, Margery combed and recombed her flip, and April looked around the inside bathroom where the nurses, or whoever it was, had individual cubbyholes. There were toothbrushes and water glasses and sanitary napkins and make-up and one had a hot water bottle, which made April laugh, thinking of some big fat nurse giving herself an enema in here. They had one at home like that, hanging on a hook behind the bathroom door. When she was little, she asked her mother why she was using it all the time, because they also had a smaller enema thing. Why did she need such a big one? Her mother told April to mind her own business. April still didn't know why ladies had to have them, and now she'd never know. She used to think eventually you'd find all these things out, but now she thought there'd always be things ahead that no one told you about and when they happened, they happened.

The last hour they spent in the lobby; not knowing it was the last hour, no one said anything. They just sat. The fact that he might be dead in there seemed a possibility and something to think about. April's face was red and her stomach felt squeezed; their mother sighed and kept recrossing her legs. She had both arms wrapped around her purse and it over her stomach like a heating pad. Margery with a dry, pale face and cold hands. By the end of the miserable hour, the thing was familiar, conversation started up on that. Facts had to be faced, their mother thought, so she presented one to see how she would do it. "Well, I don't see as he could really be doing that good now." She stopped then as the swing door opened on Dr. Whiting, still in his green surgical suit holding a sheet of paper in his hand, scanning the lobby and finding them, only after Mrs. Flanaghan was on her feet and heading in his direction, Margery in her wake, April gaping.

By the time April got there, and the doctor had waited there at the swing door because, he said, he had to get right back in there; he had already explained the situation. April found it hard to listen to the facts; there was blood on his top and down one pant's leg. She thought she might be going to gag. It was brown and dried in crusted spots. She managed to turn her eyes up to the doctor's face; he was still talking and, of course, by now they knew he was alive, but when the doctor had gone back in there, there was hardly much more. Their mother had taken a little note pad out and tried to write a few things down as soon as he was gone, but she hadn't gotten all of it and told April to hush up or she'd forget what she *did* know. They went back to the chairs and their mother kept asking the same questions; she was right there, April thought, how come she hadn't gotten the story straight?

72

"You're no good at all," her mother said to April, when she saw the younger one had picked up not a single fact during all that time standing there, and her with the good memory they were always hearing about. Margery, thank God, she told everyone afterward, was the only one with her wits about her, who managed to get the story straight at all, and they made her tell it a few times, till the two of them, April and her mother, could picture it, awful as it was. After that, whenever her mother retold the story, and there were a lot of phone calls that night, she used the exact words Margery had used, and Margery, April noticed, although she didn't know how she had noticed because she hadn't heard any of it, used the words the doctor used.

The "obstruction" was the problem. The esophagus was obstructed, other things were obstructed too, and that's why he hadn't been able to eat or to hold down food he did eat. The strange part of it, the doctor—who did this kind of surgery every day—said, was how their father had caused it himself by coughing; he had coughed up his insides into his chest where they were all squashed together or something—the story got vague in here. The surgery had unobstructed, pulled down, tidied, reorganized, but, he warned, there was nothing to keep him from doing it again, and "we can't do this kind of procedure again and again, even if he had a very strong constitution, which he doesn't." He had to be kept calm, the doctor said; he has to stop drinking, and he has to stop coughing everything up. Even though only Margery heard this, the other two knew, without hearing, nothing would happen. But nobody wanted to think about that. They wanted to hear just what was done; how did he describe it again? their mother asked Margery, who spoke up loud like an authority, April thought. She could tell she was putting it on now, because they already knew everything she was going to say. It was the beginning of Margery's becoming an authority on her father's stomach trouble, an ally of her mother's to keep him on his diet and doing all the other things—or not doing them, as the case was more often—to keep him alive, or rather to keep him from letting himself die, as they accused him of wanting to do, especially now that they had the proof—Margery had it in her memory in the doctor's exact words—of how much of this he was doing to himself.

Providence, 1957:
An Accident

Reeser marked the spot on the sidewalk where his homework fell and was wrecked. How were you so dopey to drop it? Were you staring into space, looking where it was nobody's business, clumsy and stumbled on a line some fool kid had chalked for the hell of it?

It wasn't exactly a puddle it lay in, it was too flat and too even, but brown and wet with grass growing and once the homework sheet was there, the water slid into a fold and wasn't brown but clear with gray specks, but so many specks that standing up again, it was brown. The water lapped into the fold, across the middle of the page and stopped, until Reeser sunk it with his foot. The ends were still dry. He lifted it out to see what the bottom looked like, and now the ends were curling. This was just at the moment the Schaeffer blue-black began to change. First the paper was just wet, then something was happening to the 5 of 5640.2; the 5 was getting bigger, but not in an ordinary way.

"Get along with you," Mother Mary John said because, in the end, Reeser (only the boys called him Reeser, the girls called him Raymond, and that's what the nuns called him, sometimes Mister Montereesi; Raymond Montereesi is what the page said for anyone to read) left it there when other things changed, not just the 5. The page of numbers was wrecked, he told his mother, when he came home for lunch (cheese sandwich, Bosco and vanilla wafers on a Christmas napkin) with the note.

He dropped it and stood there watching; he came back on his way home for lunch, but at 3:15 when school got out and he crossed

School Street, forgetting the paper and the note, swinging his arms hard with Michael Fahey, his friend, like soldiers, their schoolbags hanging around their necks, and next thing was to pull the heavy part and hang like a dead man, he suddenly remembered and told Mikie he had to go home the other way, get a loaf of bread, see you, and it was gone. First he thought it might be blown against the fence or in the vacant lot. He forgot, thinking of the alleyway across the street, to look both ways and nearly got "clipped," as he father would say, by a light blue Plymouth, woman driver, watch where you're going, sonny. *You* watch, he said, where you're going. Are you sassing me? Don't the sisters teach you anything at school? Reeser turned his back. I'll tell your mother how you speak to me, he heard and laughed out loud: she didn't know his mother.

Where was the paper? John A. (Allen) Martin, 52 Lisbon St., Grade 4, Mother Phillip Agnes, Holy Savior School, put Raymond Montereesi's paper in a five-cent tablet with his own homework. The page was wrecked, but it wasn't dripping wet and John wondered if a dog, Rufus or King—they were close enough and he had seen them many times tearing through the field—had peed on it. He sniffed the paper, but you couldn't tell that easily. Some of the numbers, especially in the middle over the fold, were gone; there was just a clear white circle with an uneven blue border, but there on the bottom was a sum and it was wrong. John didn't fix it; he carried it to school in the afternoon and showed it to the girl, Jeanne Ann Dawley, who used to be his girlfriend and still stood by the fence separating the boys' from the girls' schoolyard to look for John in case he wanted to come over and slap hands over the top, careful not to catch hands on the pickers. Once he had stuck out his tongue and she pushed it back in his mouth with her thumb, smelled like a school-bag. Yah, he said. Yah yourself, she said, but he thought of slapping hands right away and then the bell rang, saved by the bell.

Reeser's father, who drove an oil truck for John Cola, Cola Oil, didn't see how the boy lost it, wasn't it right there in the schoolbag when he left for school? You don't just lose something, he said. Are you listening to what I'm telling you? Go easy on the boy, his mother always said, but didn't say because his father hadn't even gotten started on him yet and still had his belt on, not even reaching for it, a reasonable tone, or that's what she'd call it. A D-merit is what she said the nun had written on school stationery—Convent of the Holy Savior, 25 Regent Avenue, Mother Joseph Magdalen, FFJ, principal, Sincerely yours in Christ. What's it mean, you tell me, they going to throw you off altar boys? the father said, still reasonable. Reeser wanted to say nothing; he could also say—but sometimes it was a mistake with his father to say too much, because words tended to irritate him even more than direct disobedience, laziness or deceitfulness—he just dropped it in a puddle, but he could hear his mother opening and shutting cabinets in the kitchen, which meant she was on pins and needles herself.

He told *me*—there she was in the doorway, just in time to see the trouble start on his father's face—a dog chased him and that's why. That's why what? his father's face now right up close to his and madder than he would have been if Reeser had been ready a little earlier, not waiting so long to tell the story himself, and now the story coming out wrong, and he could see clearly from his father's face that it was wrong and that he would have to ("Control yourself, Raymond") get it beaten out of him.

You stay out of it, he said, out of the corner of his mouth, nasty the way he could be, and she flung the towel she was holding, and then slammed the bathroom door.

What the hell's wrong with you? Big Ray, as she called him to people who knew them both, father and son, gave little Ray the kind of shove that would have knocked him over if it weren't for the edge of the dining room table in the way and his hand caught in there, right where the little drawer was and the metal handle, the pain of it, though good thing his left and not the right, and she opened the door, something crashed, but Reeser was out of it. He watched his father knock—no, bang—on the closed bathroom door and they had "language"—"Don't give me your language, you lousy son of a bitch, picking on the kid day and night, I think you stink."

This was worse. Reeser took out his gum and stuck it on the top of his shoe and walked around that way; it didn't drop off until he got to the kitchen to cool his hand under the running water. It was quiet, they were quiet all of a sudden, thinking of the neighbors. His mother called his father a big bully and his father yelled he'd kick the door down; then he was crying, his father, but that was almost as bad—worse, because when his father cried, Reeser cried, too, and sometimes his mother cried. Reeser was crying in the kitchen where he couldn't hear them. He stopped crying, crying over spilled milk, picked up the gum and dropped it down the drain.

———

They had a scene, Reeser heard his mother tell Auntie Pauline the next morning. Was it the next morning that the fat kid, Joey D'Ambra, gave him back his paper? Somebody take this from you? Joey said, and Reeser didn't know what to say. Joey said: you tell me who took this here and you and me'll go beat him up like this, the fat kid said, giving Reeser a little shove to show how. Hey Reese, he said, what happened to you? Reeser looked at his hand with the bandage around the knuckles. Nothing. My eye, Joey said, your father crack you? Nope; give me that paper, Reeser said. Here, I told you I brang it to you on purpose, let's get that guy, fourth grade, I seen him, a punk.

———

A scene was what Jon Gnagy called the snow scene or the summer scene with the twisty path getting skinnier and coming to a point. Reeser couldn't get it just right, but he liked doing it anyway and his mother sometimes came and sat with him in front of the TV, peeled onions or potatoes, did spot cleaning or filed her nails. She never drew, although Reeser offered her a sheet of paper and a piece of pastel. But this wasn't the first time he'd heard his mother talk about a scene, and he knew what it meant; he didn't even look up from what he was doing—pulling the kitchen plug by its chain with the sink full of water and dishes until it made a little suck noise, then letting it drop in again. Don't do that, she said, it's little Ray, she said into the phone; he's making a noise. Oh, it's just a noise, she told Auntie Pauline in a tone, and gave him a look at the same time. He went out to the back hall and put his rubbers on. His coat was on a hook, mittens up the sleeve and a scarf on the floor laying on the boots and rubbers no one ever wore. He opened the kitchen door; his mother put her hand over the receiver; where are you going? Is it late? Listen, Paul, I've got to get the baby off, I'll call you back. Raymond. Raymond, you come back here.

———

John Martin had been showing the homework in the schoolyard. See this? I found it. What is it? I don't know, it's just arithmetic. It's subtraction, 8 take away 9, borrow 10. Keep your hands off, fatso. What'd you call me? D'you call me somethin? I didn't call you nothing. Did I call him something? I didn't call you nothing. You were talking to me before, I heard you. Was anybody talking to him? Give me that paper, I know who that is. No. Make him come and get it. Give me that paper right now—he needs it, I know this kid, he needs it. Too bad, see. John Martin's friend took it and started to rip along the fold. Hey, don't do that. Who's going to stop me? Give it to him, Danny, I don't want it. Give it to the dumbbell. What'd you call me? What'd he say to me, John, what'd he say just now?

————

Reeser had the homework in his hand. Now look what you've done, stupid. And what should he do with it? He carried it home and put it in the garbage can with the other garbage. The garbage men would see it. They wouldn't know what it was, but they'd take it anyway, they'd take anything. He put it under the string with the stack of newspapers. He folded it over so you couldn't see what it was. It would go—he had gone many times with his father—to the dump, but not to the hole, to the incinerator. Inside his schoolbag, folded in the arithmetic book, Not To Be Removed From School Premises, was tonight's homework sheet and another sheet with the extra problems, 20 subtractions altogether. If he did one subtraction in five or ten minutes, how long would it take to do 20? Reeser sat down on the porch steps and tried to do the problem mental arithmetic, then wrote it on the back of his schoolbag with ballpoint pen. He had other homework—reading and grammar. He'd never get done.

He went inside. Nobody was home; he yelled, I'm home, and no answer. Then he heard footsteps upstairs. He sat at the kitchen table and waited for her; she'd come down in a minute and make him something for a snack, then sit down and try to "pry something out of him," as he heard her tell Pauline. He'd just sit there deaf and dumb.

The Babysitter

April's father finished recuperating—he hated recuperating and tried to get back to work long before anyone thought he was ready, no one could stop him—when the lady across the street, Mrs. McManus, only married two Christmases ago, even though she was past thirty-five, had a baby. It was right before school started and you could hear it crying way down the street because Mrs. McManus, who loved to stop the neighbors coming out to hang their laundry for a chat, took it out to the porch morning and afternoon to sit on one of the green wicker rockers that came with the house (you couldn't buy them like that anymore, April's mother said). April used to see them out there from the upstairs window. The McManuses hadn't lived there long, but people knew the father-in-law, *his* father, who had been a baby doctor in the neighborhood, and popular in his day, God rest his soul. He left a nest egg, it was heard. They used it to buy the house, but the mother, very sickly, was sitting on the rest of it, they said. The two of them expected to come into it one of these days, Mrs. Dooley told the Italian lady, who mentioned it to April's mother, and it was supposed to be a tidy sum. That was an ideal (April's mother) way to make money.

April couldn't tell if she was being sarcastic because of the disappointment they had come into with her father's family, still alive and a whole neighborhood full of them in the summer colony on the south shore, but "estranged," as her mother put it, and never came around of a Sunday for a visit, which April knew they did everywhere else. "They have nothing to do with him," her mother said. "When they're thick, they're so thick, you can't break them apart come hell or high water" (and April knew she was referring to the Dooleys and things that had happened to them for all their pride: the brother killing himself, the older boy sent to jail for cheating the government, *her* father, captain of the fire department, pillar of the church, an alcoholic—people had only just found this out). And yet, the only critical remarks you heard in that house was for the woman out-of-state the brother married. "It's always outsiders," April's mother said.

They didn't think I was good enough for your father either, she said once, and April's grandmother was forever telling them why: they were from out-of-state, that was the main thing, with no father, and her on assistance when she wasn't working as a maid in other people's houses and letting the kids, his people thought, run wild. April didn't think that her mother or her aunts were that wild; they all had kids and stayed home to take care of them.

They had gone to visit his relatives once when April was a little girl. She remembered the pink and green candies on the silver saucer and the dish of ice cream in the pantry. On the way over they heard about behaving like ladies; he was all worked up because their mother wouldn't come. It was like a slap in the face, he kept saying. ("They don't want to see me. Tell them I'm laid up, tell them anything you want.") April couldn't figure out what they had done to make her mother so mad, but the grandmother said it happened before April's time. "I told them," she said, "to take good care of my little girl going so far from home." April asked what they did. "They always looked down on us." Their grandmother, a fat lady who came to their house on her bingo nights to get a ride, must have said this a million times, so April wasn't sure it was true.

The aunt warmed up a little, their father said afterward to their mother; they had started talking about old times and picture albums were dragged out of his father and mother both dead. They had taken him over to the big cupboard in the dining room, April trailing behind, and showed that his mother's china and silver, beautiful pieces she had, were all there in mint condition, polished every month, only taken out for holidays and special, they told him. The father, who was not known to criticize, kept saying how those were his mother's things from the house on Gentian Avenue, and they had no business taking over, what did they ever do for her when she was there on her sickbed all those years? "They never so much as came around to see her. Who am I to question, but I'd just like to know how they came to be entitled to her things?" Even though he was asking, April knew they weren't supposed to answer. But her mother wanted to get involved anyway; she was prepared for this conversation and it had never come up. She had a lot to say about that family, but the more she said, the less interested he seemed, and finally, because on this subject and no other she deferred to him, it was dropped. "I'm just mentioning it," he said in a sarcastic tone, "but I can't even mention things to you without you getting yourself all worked up. What do you care? It wasn't your stuff. Don't worry; I was never in a million years going to see any of it, not that there was anything so great." "You make me sick," their mother said. "You make *me* sick," he said; "why don't you get off my back?" "I'm not on your back," she said, and the subject was dropped, but she was moody all that day, and part of the next and April could tell her feelings were hurt, though she'd never in a million years admit it.

She always took that tone when the subject of the McManuses and their new baby—and all the cars parked in front of the new house, and people bounding up the stairs with presents—came up, but April didn't hold this against Mrs. McManus.

They met one afternoon after school when April was coming up the hill and Mrs. McManus (Mary, she told April her name was, but April knew she wasn't supposed to call anyone that age Mary) tried to get her attention. "Hi there," she said again, but April kept walking. "I said hi there. What are you deaf or something?" April turned, the sun right in her eyes. Mrs. McManus asked her how she was doing and if she'd like to come over and see the baby a minute, and April ran right across the street without looking. "I didn't know you were talking to me," she said, running up the stone steps. Mrs. McManus was sitting with a diaper draped over her shoulder and a bottle of formula on a dusty wood table. She had her feet up on another rocker, elastic stockings up to her knees, and loafers on. "Can you sit a minute?" April dragged a green rocker over until it was right next to

81

Mrs. McManus. "And you'd be one of the Flanaghans, I know who you are. Her name is Patty." She turned the baby around so April could see the face, but there wasn't much to see: it had straight black hair and a red mark on its cheek where it was mashed against its mother's side. "Patricia Elizabeth." April said she thought Patty was cute. "Do you like babies?" the lady said, laying the baby down again across her lap. "Of course you do," she answered for April. "Patricia—that was the name I picked as a novice. You knew I was in the convent? I was in almost four years. I didn't want to leave," she went on; "they told me my health wasn't good enough."

"This isn't so bad, though, is it?" she said, and April wondered if she meant *this*—right now—or just Patty.

"My whole name was Sister Patricia Hanley—Hanley is my maiden name—and Elizabeth is for my mother, Elizabeth Ann McNamara that was, and this one is Patty McManus." "Cute," April said again, sitting back in her chair and nearly going all the way over, but Mrs. McManus caught the rocker in time by the arm. "Aren't these chairs something?" she said. "I hate them, but we're going to hang onto them for now. After all, we got them for 'no.' "

The lady chatted like no one had ever chatted with April, until five o'clock when the chimes went off in the house and Mrs. McManus said she'd have to be going. "Don't be a stranger," she said to April. "Don't wait for a formal invitation. I'm out here every day with her. We might even have you over to sit some time. Tell your mother Mary McManus was asking for her."

"Guess where I've been!" April screamed as soon as she was inside the door.

It didn't take long before April knew all the ins and outs of the Hanley family, Mary McManus's mother and dad and four sisters and who they were all married to, and where they lived, how old their kids were and how they all spent their summers together at Misquamicut State Beach. There was a nephew a year older than April coming on for Thanksgiving and a plan was made to go to the drive-in, the whole family, and April. Mainly April heard about the wonderful time Mary had had in high with her sisters and a million friends and how they'd gotten away with murder ("I was smoking in the seventh grade") because she had her license and could borrow her father's car at the drop of a hat to cart the nuns wherever they wanted to go—to the religious good store, to the dentist; plus she was related by marriage to the McInerneys, who *owned* the religious goods store. "We were always raising hell," Mrs. McManus told April while they sat drinking instant coffee in the kitchen with a box of Gorman's donuts open between them. Mary McManus had offered her coffee the second time she came over and April had been taking a cup ever since, with three sugars and milk. Mrs. McManus would drink three or four cups to keep her throat from getting too dry, she said, but April only drank half of hers because it would stunt (the grand-mother) her growth.

When Mary McManus got up to go to the bathroom, April took the chance to look around. It was a funny house, the kind of house her mother would detest, everything so dark and gloomy. The woodwork, even in the kitchen, was dark brown, shiny with varnish. The kitchen walls were wallpapered yellow and red with stripes and flowers and bumpy wall under that. There was a brown dinette with chrome legs and yellow plastic-covered chairs. The linoleum was so worn out you couldn't tell its color, but it was checkered in something.

Refrigerator in the back hall and all the china cupboards flush with the ceiling, impossible to reach the top shelf. Mrs. McManus had two stepstools, one in front of the sink, an old-fashioned sink with pipes visible and a basin on the floor to catch the leaks. But the curtains, April told her mother, were pretty—yellow dotted swiss café cur-tains, but underneath were dark green shades and not a single Venetian blind in the whole house. It sounded (April's mother) hideous. The rest of the house wasn't hideous, said April, it was beautiful. "I bet."

Mahogany dining room table with the lace tablecloth and the ashtrays with silver rims, the TV with remote control buttons and the gold brocade sofa, tassels on the cushions even. "It doesn't sound comfortable," April's mother said, but she agreed with the plan to take a look herself when April went to sit the first time, a week from Friday, when the McManuses were going to a double shower for a cousin in Cranston; she was always going somewhere, April said, but he stayed home; this time, they were going together.

Mr. McManus—people around the neighborhood who didn't automatically call him Bob, called him "the husband"—was a surprise to everybody because he was so handsome. April's mother said it didn't matter what he looked like because he was such a stick. April thought her mother was being too critical. When they went over to the housewarming, her mother had nothing but good to say. Her impressions changed and a week later, she said they were typical Irish, all front. *She* was alright, talk your ear off, but down to earth, ordinary; he was a cold fish, no personality, no fun.

April didn't think being stiff took away from how cute he was with his brown eyes and curly hair. The first night she babysat, she looked at the wedding album and the pictures on the wall, the christening pictures in a silver bowl on the buffet, too. She didn't understand, she told her mother, what he saw in her, Mary McManus, who even in her heyday looked old, much older than him and exhausted. You could tell she was overweight in her wedding gown with its tight sleeves and full skirt. The only thing that made them look married, April thought, was their feet: his shiny black shoe and her white spike heel next to each other, almost touching, in the back of the limousine, the sight of which gave April goose bumps in a way that the kiss on the eighth page near the wedding cake didn't—that looked like the kind people called a smooch, plus Mary McManus had turned her face so all you saw was jaw. April didn't get anything out of that, even though she looked at it a long time sitting on the couch in the quiet house. She put the book away a few minutes and tried looking at it again fresh. There was nothing in it at all; there was nothing in their going off together to the shower either, him in a navy blue suit, her in a light green brocade dress with cap sleeves, hat and a veil. He opened the front door and went out first, she followed, coming back in again to tell April about the candy in the silverware drawer and the bottle of Coke in the refrigerator. April didn't understand how she could take him for granted and look so dowdy. She herself always felt formal with him and acted formal because he looked like he appreciated formality, a quality he could never get from Mary. She looked at the wedding album again and was just about to get up for the candy when there was a noise. She tried to get the big square book under the coffee table. Someone was tapping on the window. It was just her mother.

Margery was with her. "Hurry up," she said, as soon as April got the door open, "or someone will see us out here."

April showed them the kitchen and the baby's room. Her mother said she hated the idea of the refrigerator in the back hall; the dark woodwork was bad enough. Worse was when she opened the refrigerator and saw what was in there: bottle of Coke, three eggs and a head of lettuce—wilted—ketchup, mustard—the cheap kind. "She doesn't leave you much, does she?" It came up several times at home, too, when she criticized April's "friend" for being so cheap she didn't even leave a few crumbs for the babysitter.

The baby was already asleep but the visitors weren't interested anyway; they had already seen the baby. They were interested in the dining room and the living room, because everything was brand new and fancy. You can tell there's a little money here, April's mother said. She admired the table and the buffet, the gold sofa too, although it wasn't the kind of thing she'd run right out and buy herself. Margery turned the TV on with the remote-control button and they all sat down and watched "To Tell the Truth." Their mother said she couldn't stay; she had left him in bed and the phone might ring, so she'd just sit a minute. They watched that show and another show came on, but Margery got up, put the remote control unit in an ashtray and said she was going. "Don't you want to see what's in here?" April said, jumping up for the wedding book.

Margery and her mother tried to get the book away from April, but she insisted on sitting between them so she could explain. They couldn't see good that way, so they pushed the coffee table out and had April sit on the floor.

Margery said she didn't think he was that good looking, judging from the pictures, more corny looking. He's not my type either, her mother said; I've met him and he's a nothing; she's got a lot more life in her, although all that talk gets on your nerves. They were crazy, April said, he was a living doll. She couldn't see what he saw in *her*, though.

"What's wrong with her?" the mother said. She wasn't bad, Margery said. Older looking, that's all, the mother said, plus she's got enough personality for both of them.

"And I thought she was such a good friend of yours," their mother added a minute later. "Yeah, who are you to criticize?" Margery said.

April said she liked her as a person, it wasn't that. "Well, maybe *he* likes her as a person," Margery said and they laughed. "We really got her going," their mother said to Margery.

"Lay down on the couch," April's mother said as they were leaving; "they don't expect you to wait up for them. If I can't get you up tomorrow on time, you're not doing this again."

———

April looked at the christening pictures again after they left. There was another tap at the window—Margery, carrying a brown bag. "Here," when April opened the door, "Ma says not to go hungry." Margery turned right around again. "I got to go, Eddie's supposed to call."

April found a ham sandwich on a snowflake roll—the rolls her mother usually saved for her father's lunch because he had started not eating again and she was trying to make the food more appealing. A lot of good it does, she told April, he gives it away, I know he does—Oreos wrapped in wax paper and a banana. There was a napkin in there, all wrinkled on the bottom. This might have been his lunch, it was exactly what he got. April put the bag in the refrigerator, took out the cookies, and watched "Dr. Kildare" and the "Westinghouse Playhouse," then ate the sandwich and drank the Coke right out of the bottle.

———

They were talking again in Mrs. McManus's kitchen; the baby had been put to bed. Mrs. McManus already asked April, who had turned thirteen her last birthday, if she had been on her first date yet, and April told her again no. But she had been to some boy-girl dances at St. John's, and almost fixed up once at the end of last summer with a blind date.

Everything was planned, her friend Cynthia's date even had a car and drove, and the guy was supposed to call her the day before to tell her the time. But it had fizzled out because the boy couldn't get the car after all; instead they were going to meet at the high school tennis court and talk, maybe go up to the Cottage for a Coke. April and Cynthia wore their madras shorts, long-sleeved blouses and April put her wallet in Cynthia's ditty bag.

At first they just talked—they met the boys at the gate and April didn't think her date was cute at all, but he dressed sharp in chinos and loafers and looked older because of the smell of aftershave—and April could tell right away he didn't like her, right from the beginning things didn't go right. Cynthia and Timmy left right away to take a walk across the football field. Donald—that was the guy's name—told April he thought Cynthia was a cute girl and did she see those trees over there by the fence? Behind those trees were benches where you could have some privacy because no one could see you from the street. That's where they were going, he said. April wondered whether she was supposed to go there too, but he didn't move; he didn't do anything at all. He told April about the car he wanted to get, and was going to get pretty soon, without once looking at her, or asking her a single thing about herself like they were supposed to; then he said he had to go because of a phone call he was waiting for. "Tell them I had to go, will you?"

But April didn't wait to tell them. She couldn't even buy herself an ice cream on the way home because Cynthia had her wallet. She knew what this was: this was the shaft. She saw Cynthia at church the next day. She kept talking about what a good time they had had and how Donald had liked her a lot and if she wanted to go in the car to bowl sometime, they could go.

April didn't know whether to believe her or not, she told Mrs. McManus, but nothing came of it anyway. So she wasn't sure, she said, when people asked if she had had a date, whether to say yes or no. Margery seemed to think she had. April told her the day after, leaving some details out, and Margery accused her of making out on the first date.

But Mrs. McManus pooh-poohed her experience. Just wait, she said, till my nephew gets here; things will get better. He's cute, she said, and you're cute, plus you're just about the same age. I can hardly wait, she said, twisting around in her chair to pull a teaspoon from out of the drawer behind her. "You can come down to the beach house. We have plenty of room. Someone will keep an eye on you, don't worry; we won't let the two of you spend all your time together." But they could all go to the drive-in together in the station wagon and eat popcorn and have a hell of a time. She might even be able to talk Mr.

McManus into coming, although he loves his home, she said; we can hardly get him out of it. He's not like me; I love to go.

"I bet I never told you," Mrs. McManus said after she brought the boiling kettle to the table and filled the cups, and pulled out a package of family-sized filled cookies, the cheap kind April's mother bought, "how Bob and I met and got married." April had heard it before, but no, she was dying to hear it, she said. "Well," Mrs. Manus said, pouring milk into her cup and April's and setting the carton on the table, "you think he's shy now. He wasn't a bit shy then—just the opposite. I had been out of the convent exactly two months—I remember because it was the month before Christmas and I had come out September 21st. I'll never forget that day. A group of us were going to the Shamrock Inn for a drink: my sister, my sister's boy-friend, Leo McAloon—he works for the state now, but he was just out of the service then and full of pep—two of my cousins from down the line, and my friend Louise Goggin and my other sister, Ann Mary, the one who lives in New Jersey. Well, we got there—Louise had an old Buick—and they're playing a little music and right off the bat we run into a nice bunch of guys, who tell us how they all work for the state and maybe Leo already knew them, I don't know, and don't you know they sit right down with us at a table and before you know it we're all up dancing.

"They had a nice crowd out there in those days, fun, no toughs. Anyway, who should ask me to dance but Bob McManus of all people. We danced a couple of dances and sat out a few and got to talking. We had a friend or two in common, you know how it is. My father knew a lot of people in his time down there." She stopped a minute, leaned forward. "*You* think he's shy but do you know what he said to me that first night? Right there at the Shamrock Inn? He said, how does it happen that a girl like you is still single? Can you picture that? Can't get two words out of him now. Well," leaning back, "he's always told me how he knew what he wanted, he was just waiting around to find it and scoop it up, which is what he did.

"I told him that night how I'd been out two months—not quite two months—but before that I was two years in the convent and he wanted to know the ins and outs, where, what order, where I'd gone to high. Well, before you know it, he's asking me out to a time they were having at Holy Savior here, because he was from your parish. It was a ham and bean supper, all married couples, families. A little on the stodgy side, but guess what?" Mrs. McManus took a chocolate sandwich cookie and pushed the bag toward April, who was trying to lose weight—Margery had said this was the main reason the blind date hadn't worked out, when April finally broke down and told her the story—but Mrs. McManus kept pushing them. "Come on, don't let me eat these alone." April took a cookie and tried to make it last, so she wouldn't end up eating a whole row to keep up with Mary McManus.

So, they did this together and did that together, and Bob Mc-Manus eventually met the family and they all liked him on the spot. His father being a doctor, and a state medical examiner, didn't hurt one bit, she said. This was the part of the story Mary McManus went on and on about: what this relative said, what they did Christmas eve, Christmas day to divide the time equally between the two families. It was that Christmas, she said, that he "threw the purple rock," as Mr. McManus put it himself. He didn't put it that way to her, she said, he just gave it. He put it to a mutual friend, who asked when Bob was going to throw the white rock, and he said pretty soon, I just threw the purple rock.

April had never heard it put this way before, but she was sure it showed the same feeling as the shoes did, but in a different way. She could hardly pay attention to the rest of the story; she kept thinking about the rings being tossed in a lap. She explained to Margery that he wouldn't have to have said a thing; in this way, people like him had the advantage over talkers. Margery said she had never heard of it before, and it didn't sound romantic one bit; it sounded like he was just trying to get out of it. If she was this dense, April said, there was no need to explain any more.

April heard Margery using the expression later on with one of her friends, when they were walking down to the Art Cleansers and April had tagged along. Margery let her come, but the two friends only talked to each other. April laughed when she heard the white rock thrown into the conversation. Margery explained it to her friend, who liked the idea of it, neither one of them saying anything about how it was hard or cold-blooded.

———

He threw the white rock in February around Valentine's Day, Mrs.
McManus said, and this was the point where the story always began
to wind down—or wind back. Sometimes she started again at an
earlier point and worked her way back with a different set of circumstances: her father's heart attack, her job as a secretary at the suit
factory, her best friend's engagement. "I knew he was going to," she
said, "but I didn't know when." It was a Friday night and they had
gone to a show at the Palace and out for a drink at the Davenport
Lounge downtown. "I got up to go to the ladies' room," Mrs.
McManus said, looking out the window all of a sudden where
something had caught her eye, but April saw it was just the boy next
door carrying a watering can to the backyard, "and when I came
back, this little box"—she turned from the window, where they both
watched Terrence Dooley water a forsythia bush near the garage, and
showed April how big it was by making a square with her thumbs and
forefingers, "about yea-big, right next to my water glass. It was on the
napkin. I pretended not to notice it," she said, "but I could see it all
the way from the ladies' room." They turned to watch Terry carrying
the watering can back into the house. "I think he's awfully cute,"
Mrs. McManus said, "do you girls know him at all?" April said she
knew him, but not that well. "I see him at the nine on Sundays," said
Mrs. McManus taking another cookie, "and he's so cute in his
cassock. You girls don't like him, though?" April wondered if she
wanted to get right into this subject, but before she decided to start
into how long she'd been liking Terrence Dooley, how she kept
watch on the window she knew was his, how they had signals—she
and Sally Dooley—so April would know if he were home or not, Mrs.
McManus moved back into the story again. "So, he just pointed at it.
Aren't you going to open this and see what's in it? he said. I turned
forty shades of red," Mrs. McManus said and April could see even
now her neck was getting red. "But I managed to get it open, and
guess what?"

They could see Terry through the living room window now, and
there was Mrs. Dooley. Was she yelling, or just talking? Now they
couldn't see him. "If I were your age, that's the kind I'd go for," Mrs.
McManus said. "A lot of girls in my grade," April said, "think he's a
doll." "From what I (Mrs. McManus) hear he's going in to be a priest;
is that the story?"

April didn't think she should spread it around that he had a girlfriend and went to make-out parties. Nobody was supposed to know. She remembered the eighth-grade graduation party. He came over to her group. She couldn't believe he was going to talk to her. She could smell something on his breath, and she had been watching him over on the couch with Marcia McLaughlin. "Hey," he said, "how're you doing?" The Dooleys were always very polite, so April tried to be polite too, although she knew he was only talking to her so she wouldn't run right home and tell her mother.

Her mother could have cared less what he did, April thought; she liked the kids to have a good time, she was always saying. But April thought better of mentioning it to Mrs. McManus, even though she seemed so young. She had a lot of respect for vocations and deep down, April figured, wouldn't like it one bit.

It was getting dark outside and Mrs. McManus said she'd better get started peeling potatoes. She told April she could stay, but April said she had her own potatoes to peel, and went home.

Providence, 1948:
The Most Complimentary Thing

Uncle Billy started out getting straight A's. He was so underweight, couldn't even finish a popsicle by himself, and a crybaby. His mother (big Aunt Helen) never let him out of her sight. He came after the others: Bobby, Ellen, Ted, Mikey and Alice had grown up and married, one of them dead, and kids of their own and Auntie Helen with no one at home but the baby.

I got straight A's just like Uncle Billy, they said in a warning tone, but I wasn't a bit like Uncle Billy, who had gone mental long before I even went to school to get them. Still people saw the resemblance.

When I look at the pictures of Uncle Billy, old or young, I can't believe they sent him to school. There he is with Aunt Helen—they're both dead now—holding his hand in a long pink glove and he has that grin on his face that runs in the family and means imbecile. I think of Uncle Billy behind that smile and all the harsh words it brought him. I have exactly the same face.

But this isn't our connection, although I doubt anyone could resist, once seen, an imitation of Uncle Billy's gift face. You were either on one side of it or the other.

Aunt Helen's other kids didn't have it, but none of them had straight A's in grade two and then the ungraded room and put in the institution for life. I see their pictures, the girls with overhanging brows that also ran in the family and the boys with goony grins of their own, but not like Billy's, looking inside and out at the same time. There were so many of them all of once, they didn't get to hold that pink glove like Billy did, plus the father, Uncle Frank, was in the picture then, too, tall, a saintly—they said—man with buck teeth. No, they didn't have the chances Billy had, home all alone with Helen, her last baby, the pride and joy.

————

What did they do all those afternoons? Big Aunt Helen never went out; you never saw her on the avenue. She listened to Sunday Mass on the radio coming direct from the cathedral, had the groceries delivered and kept two sets of curtains on the windows—plus the shades—with her and Billy planked at the kitchen table looking through the cracks down to the side street and the neighbors' backyards. She never missed a trick, my mother would tell me. My father indicated Uncle had gotten what they call an "earful." Was it the earful that did it?

When I was little (little Mary, they called me), my father took me to visit Aunt Helen, but Uncle Billy was already gone. I saw a picture of him that was pasted inside a kitchen cabinet so nobody could see it unless you went looking for it. The only thing I could see wrong with the picture was instead of a belt, Uncle Billy was holding up his pants with a rope, and the tee shirt he always wore and slippers. The rope didn't look right, which was why Aunt Helen, who was still proud of her Billy—the best-looking one of all, she said; I remember her saying it—hid it away. He was big and fat by then with a short haircut, almost no hair, and all his teeth gone.

In my picture, which I never tried to destroy, around the Uncle Billy smile is another smile: I was that fat. My ears are covered by flaps of hair, but the earful could still get through.

————

What else did they do in the afternoons but sit together with Aunt Helen telling Uncle Billy the mistakes that were out there to be made—she had seen them all—if he wanted to make them: it was his choice. She, to keep from making any (and as far as she was concerned, she hadn't yet, although Frank had), was keeping close to home, watching out the window to remind herself, and Uncle Billy right beside her, of their variety, in case they forgot they were still human like the neighbors so obviously were.

So Uncle Billy went out that one year to make his marks in grade two: an A for each endeavor, but given this perfection (and Aunt Helen had kept the report card in with the marriage license and the deed to the house), decided not to mar it, and started being absent.

———

I remember in seventh grade—I was in seventh—he was out for summer vacation; every year he took one, up until the time Aunt Helen died, and then he just stayed up there in the institution until he died himself. Wading in the ocean sometimes his trunks would come unbuttoned and someone would have to run in and get Aunt Helen or Cousin Eddie, who took care of him. He's unbuttoned himself, was the way they put it, and I knew what they meant by "himself." But this was not a sin because, although it was grown-up, poor Uncle Billy was like a little baby.

I would never let my bathing suit come undone. He would stand there in the ocean grinning and dangle—this is a word I would only use now when I can't picture it anymore; then I wouldn't use any word because I went blind seeing.

He sat at the dinner table with us and Cousin Eddie cut up his meat. Sometimes cried while he ate or dribbled food on his bib, but little girls and young ladies were not gaping. Aunt Helen, if she caught my eye, would rub the side of her nose to remind me about "nose trouble." Nothing Uncle Billy did was of interest to children. I tried to act like it wasn't but sometimes had to shut my eyes to keep them from "revolving."

———

So there were the two things we had in common: straight A's and the earful, because Uncle Billy never had nose trouble, and Auntie Helen kept him from everything else. They sat by the window drinking a cup of tea. Next door was Mrs. Hanrahan, a widow, who liked to sit on the narrow strip of concrete in her backyard shaded by the house and read old movie magazines. Aunt Helen and Mrs. Hanrahan never spoke; Aunt Helen felt the woman was beneath her, plus the husband had been known to play the horses. The lady directly behind, Mrs. Francazio, tending an ailing husband and a beautiful flower garden and those skinny Italian tomatoes Aunt

Helen had to throw out because you couldn't slice them up for a BLT and they didn't taste right, plus Italian. Kitty-corner was a young couple, Ed and Frances Gilfillan, pillars of the church, people said, but Aunt Helen said they had their problems too, just like everyone else: I hear them at night having words. The Gilfillans, feeling Aunt Helen's restless eyes and the "backward boy" up there with her— everyone could see them, this is what my mother said, big as life up there, although they thought they were invisible—kept their Venetian blinds, all white except the green one in the bathroom, shut tight. Lights on half the night, Aunt Helen told my father, but no air coming through those windows unless it was a sweltering hot day. You can't tell me, Jimmy, they don't have something to hide. There were others Aunt Helen could see or hear, if she and Uncle Billy moved to another window and tried to peer through the sides of the curtains. And the way people live, she would tell Uncle Billy, makes you sick.

Billy, my mother said, could have taken care of her in her old age, if they hadn't forced him out. This I never understood because it wouldn't have been Aunt Helen who forced him. She liked having him there: he would dust a little and it was his job to empty the trash in the bin and bring up the coal in the winter. People spoke to him on the street: hi there, Billy, they said, and he always spoke back. He took off his cap when he passed the church. Doing what I always did—peek through the bushes in the back of the schoolyard—I saw him once; there he was walking down the street, not in the middle, but not in the gutter either, all by himself, and not going in the direction of Aunt Helen's. I mentioned it at home to my mother; she said she'd heard he liked to get out and wander. He went as far as downtown one day ("235 Regent Avenue? We got a Billy here, Ma'am, found him out behind the Outlet warehouse wandering"). Someday, my mother said, he's going to get lost and never come back.

The whole family on my father's side had gone to Holy Savior Grammar and they were always telling me, the nuns, how I was smart like this one, or not smart like that one, but they didn't mention Uncle Billy at all and he had done so well with them. People thought it was a bad boy hit him hard on the head, banged his head on the bubbler in the Boys' Basement, that's what must have done it because no on in the family EVER. In the fourth grade I threw a rock at a boy's head because of dirty looks and he ran home crying. But Uncle Billy wasn't a bully, he never picked on little kids even when he was a grown-up. That stupid grin made people so mad, slap it right off him, but he doesn't know any better. Aunt Helen was the only one it didn't bother; she said it reminded her of the sweet face of Jesus.

Mair—ee, he would say to me, when they told him my name. They also said he didn't know what he was saying, but it seemed to me, a big girl, he knew.

At Uncle Billy's wake. The family was there and Uncle Billy dressed in a nice blue suit; it didn't look like him. I wore a navy blue dress and people told me to look alive, but it wasn't sad I was feeling. He had a life, people said, Helen took good care of him, she loved him like a baby and when she couldn't take care of him any more, he got the best of care and beautiful grounds to walk on. I didn't have any feelings about Uncle Billy; I was in ninth grade, fat and homely and people thought mental, too. Someone had done it to Billy when he was a little boy. How had I done it? By staring, by being interested in what didn't concern me, by being too critical, and just by looking mental. People would go on that alone, I knew that much, if they had to.

I shook hands with all the friends of the family and sat quietly in my seat without tapping my foot or doing something flighty with my hands. Later, at Aunt Mae's house, I ate a sandwich and reached for another, but even before they told me, I knew not to act like a pig with poor Uncle Billy not cold in his grave yet. I ate a cake instead with white frosting and jelly on the inside; I felt I had made a mistake picking that one instead of a pastry, so I took two. Nobody noticed. No one wanted to talk to a big gawky thing like me, so I just sat and thought about Uncle Billy, a jerk his whole life and he didn't even know it.

I was overhearing how Billy, although he made his First Confession, had no stain of sin on his soul—except, I felt like saying, the ones he committed in grade two when he was normal. Aunt Margaret had that old brown dress she wore to all the weddings and funerals, trying to tell an in-law what not to think about poor Uncle Billy; he had his problems, we all have our problems, but think what a spanking clean soul he could bring to St. Peter.

You don't think he'll have to do any Purgatory? I head Adeline, Teddy's wife, say. I'm not saying that, but I think they'd put him in Limbo with the lost souls rather than in Purgatory with the sinners. With the babies in Limbo? Adeline said. Oh, don't ask me, Adeline, I'm not up on it; I do know you'll be getting the benefit to pray for his soul because he won't need it. I hope he's thinking of me, Margaret in her wrinkled dress said, hoping to be contradicted, and old Helen, too—nobody's *that* perfect.

That's when they saw me looking. Well, what do you think, Mary Mahoney, you're so smart in school, where do you think your Uncle Billy is? Depends, I said, not wanting to say anything fresh and something right there on the tip of my tongue, plus there was Fr. Conlon ready to say the rosary for stainless Uncle Billy, who didn't need it, but the rest of them did, that's what I was thinking.

They were proud of their stains, and dead Uncle Billy was even more of a jerk for not having any; worse, not having the ability to have any.

Don't confuse stains with mistakes, Aunt Helen would have whispered to Uncle Billy, if they had been at the wake; mistakes were what people knew you were doing; stains were things only God knew, which people could have known, but they didn't, because you were careful to hide them.

And nobody shed a tear because they were glad God took him in the end, poor thing. He looked like a man in his casket, which surprised me; it made me think maybe he was normal all along and nobody knew it. But I had seen him up at the institution those Sundays shaking his head back and forth, big and empty like Humpty Dumpty. They had him in a one-piece green suit, loose and wrinkled and paper slippers. Lying in the casket, there was no backwardness on his face; they had shut the mouth, fixed the skin so it wasn't lapping over the sides, even the flattop had grown out a little and was combed with a part, so—except for being fatter—he looked just like Uncle Bobby at Uncle Bobby's wake. Everyone mentioned how natural he looked, but I knew that meant unnatural because he didn't look like himself, which was the most complimentary thing you could say at a wake: he looks so much like himself, Catherine, but no one said this about Billy because this would have made mock of the whole thing, and this is what people are afraid of in a wake: mockery, so everyone—even the ones who'd had a few too many—were careful to behave themselves like they were in church, the temptation was so great.

I started out, I remember, saying something about Uncle Billy's report card. I never saw it, but it was still being talked about when I was a little girl, and I tried to picture it: a yellow card like a multiplication table: William F. Doyle, Grade 2, Mother Philomena (still there when I went). Catechism: A, Arithmetic: A, Reading: A, Penmanship: A, Civics: A, Spelling: A, English Grammar: A, Art: A, Deportment: A, Effort: A. Respectfully yours in Christ, Mother Philomena, F.F.J. Everybody thought of it as Uncle Billy's best year, and how far he could have gone in life if God hadn't given his poor mother the cross he gave her to bear was anybody's guess, but someone always whistled through their teeth to show just how far. He had the brain, I always heard this; I knew what the rest of it was, although no one ever said it: he had the brain, but he abused it.

———

My report card, up until now, has always been AAAAAAAAA AAAAAA, maybe an A- for Deportment because of idle chatter. But they don't talk about this as my gift because there are too many report cards and years and how can anything be that great if it's always the same? Uncle Billy paid for his year, but I haven't paid for mine yet, and people are waiting for me to take a tumble, as they say, even though this is only ninth grade and I've got my whole life ahead of me. If it was good enough for Aunt Helen's—God rest his soul—baby boy, it's good enough for me, but I'm still not as mental as I'm going to be.

Margery's Prom

It was two days later, a Saturday, that Mrs. McManus called the house and told April she had already talked to her mother and it was all right for April to sit that night and stay over; the McManuses were going to a party way up in Tiverton and wouldn't be back till late. "You can sit and watch TV until you get tired; I'll make up the cot."

When April got off the phone, she went into the dark living room, all the blinds shut, and opened an old *Life* magazine. April? Are you finished with the phone? If you are, you can get yourself back up here; you're not done yet. April folded the magazine so she could find her page and stuck it into the back of the rack.

"Ma," standing behind her mother who was scrubbing the bathroom floor. What? "Mrs. McManus wants me to sit and stay over." I know. Her mother switched from the scrub brush to the sponge to mop up the gray water on the tiles. I talked to her yesterday. Make sure you have a decent pair of pajamas and see if Margery will let you take her robe. If she won't, you can take mine, but don't get it all sweaty. She finished with the floor and handed April the pail of dirty water to throw down the downstairs toilet.

When April came back with the empty pail, her mother was in her bedroom standing in front of the mirror putting in pin curls. "I think she likes you, Mary McManus does," pulling a pink nylon cap over the pin curls. "She's always telling me what a nice girl you are. She thinks you're *so* friendly. You're not so friendly around here. Always got a face on you—same goes for that one in there," pointing to Margery's room. "You're all nice on the outside and rotten at home. You get that from him, not me."

99

April's mother pointed to the other side of the bed where she wanted her to go help with the clean sheets. She thought she heard April say she wasn't the grouchy one. "Oh no, you're cheerful all the time. We can always tell when you're home, you're so cheerful." Her mother went to throw the dirty sheets down the stairs to be washed in the second load. When she got back, April had climbed on the bed for a rest. "You should see your face right now if you think you're so cheerful. You look like an undertaker." That made April laugh and she moved so she could see herself laugh in the mirror, but her mother said to cut the comedy and finish tucking in.

Margery had gotten out of all the work because she and Ellen McGovern were going to Fall River to the dress mills to shop for prom gowns. April didn't think it was fair; her mother said her time would come and Margery would have to stay home. "She'll be married then," April said, "with a hundred kids, and then they'll be nobody home to help." "Too bad," Margery, getting dressed in her room.

Don't feel bad, little girl, April's mother said, she'll have her own housework to do then and a houseful of screaming brats.

"Like hell I will."

Margery was going to the prom with Eddie McLaughlin, Rita McLaughlin's son from Harold Street. Mr. Flanaghan had gone to school with Rita's sister, Alice. A nice family, he told Margery several times, but she didn't like the family at all. There was just the mother who lived in a second-floor tenement and worked at Bell's drugstore part-time. Margery had never been to the house, but she was always bumping into Mrs. McLaughlin on the avenue, who went out of her way to be as friendly as she could be, but Margery could tell how phony it was. The mother had told Eddie several times to tell the Flanaghan girl she was dying to see her dress and to make sure to stop by on their way to the high school. "She just wants to see," Margery told her mother, "if I look tough like the girls at the public." Mrs. Flanaghan thought this was funny, but warned Margery to pick out a nice gown and not something cheap looking, and not to go over twenty or she'd have to pay it back. "Make sure you buy something your father will like," as Margery was leaving. "He doesn't like anything." "Just do it."

100

April was surprised to see she was in such a good mood after having to shell out money for a prom gown. "Get the money from my budget," she told Margery, then sent April into her room to "pick up the clutter before I get in there with the vacuum. And don't forget under the bed where you're trying to hide everything."

———

At 7:30 April carried Margery's overnight case, a present she picked out for herself when it was her turn to have the green stamps, across the street to the McManuses. She brought her geometry book, a pad to write letters and one of the novels her grandmother had left in the bookcase downstairs, the story of Conrad Hilton. She didn't know who Conrad Hilton was, but her grandmother had told them what a good story it was and how she remembered him in Chicago when she was just married marching down a parade in his silver Rolls Royce. The book was so old the pages were falling out. April's mother, who hated trash like this, said it didn't belong in her house—because it had a picture, April figured, of Mrs. Hilton on the cover in a white strapless sheath and a hotel behind her—had thrown it in the garbage, but April pulled it out when she was emptying the baskets. She kept it hidden in her sock drawer and then transferred it to the overnight case.

He answered the door in his black suit and barefoot, no socks. The baby was crying, and he explained, holding the door open for her, that Mrs. McManus—they always called each Mr. and Mrs.—went early with her sister to pick up an order from the caterers, and that he was going to follow them. He told her to come out to the kitchen if she wanted to, he was heating a bottle for the baby. April sat down at the kitchen table, and when the milk was heated she offered to take it in to the baby. "Oh don't stand there and hold it. There's a holder in there if you can find it. I'm just going to put my shoes on. Come back and sit with me a minute."

The baby was already asleep. "She's tired," Mr. Manus, coming into the baby's room behind April. "Mrs. had her out all afternoon downtown looking for a dress." He took the bottle and carried it to the kitchen. "Will this keep?" April said she didn't know, although she thought it might be something she should know. "Never mind; I'll pour it out."

101

"Sit down a minute and keep me company. I don't have to go for another twenty minutes. Unless you want to watch TV. Did you bring your homework? What's that book I saw you carrying?"

April had forgotten who it was the book was about, somebody famous. She was going to get up to show him but he said never mind, it didn't matter. She was surprised he could be so friendly; he had never been friendly before. He asked her about school and got up to pour her a Coke, but she drank it too fast, got bubbles up her nose. He stood up and asked her if she was all right or should be slap her on the back. It seemed to give him a scare because he got right up after and went to the bedroom; looking for his shoes, he said. Then he got his topcoat out and laid it over the back of the chair. "I've got to get going in a minute." He sat down again. "It's going to be a long night, but we like these people. Haven't seen *her* in ages, nice people. Do you know where you're going to sleep? She just changed the sheets the other day and you'll be real comfortable. I've slept there myself, nice comfortable bed. Don't wait up for us, go to bed when you feel like it."

He went into the baby's room again. April followed him to the doorway to hear what he was saying. "You'll be all right, won't you?" squeezing past April to get back to the kitchen. "Good," he said, lifting his coat off the chair. "You're in charge." He gave April a little pat on the shoulder. "Don't forget to lock up when I leave, and don't let anyone in. But *you* know that." He still didn't leave. He stayed a few more minutes. "Will you be all right now?"

When he was gone April went to the bathroom mirror to see how she looked. The bathroom light was glary and there was a speck of lipstick and one of toothpaste on the mirror. She looked exactly the same, pimples, eyes half closed, glasses slipping down her nose, hair couldn't be flatter. She looked in the medicine chest to see if there was anything to put on. There was just the one lipstick, and that was the phone ringing.

Just her mother checking to see if everything was all right, had they gone, did she want any company, was she scared? April didn't know whether she wanted any or not, maybe not right that minute. Her mother said she and Margery would be coming right over, and did they leave anything to eat?

April sat on the couch and looked at the cover of the wedding book for a minute before pulling it out like she knew she would. The first picture she knew by heart: Mary McManus fixing her veil in the mirror. Skipped over a few and there the two of them were in the car. She picked the remote control unit out of the silver ashtray and turned the set on—"Carol Burnett." She put a pillow over her face and screamed until her glasses got foggy. Had something happened or hadn't it? It had.

———

The prom was only a week away and Margery, with the pale yellow organza gown, very youthful and sweet, even her mother thought, was writing a list similar to one she had seen in the magazines of things to do during the week before to make sure everything went okay with no surprises. She had given Eddie the color of the gown and exactly the kind of colonial bouquet of yellow roses, or daisies if yellow roses were too high, that would go with it. She wanted to ask him what florist he was planning to go to, but her mother told her that was a little pushy in her book. "Let him make his own decision without you leading him by the nose." Margery's mother had drawn the conclusion from this and other little things that Margery was none too crazy about this boy. If she was, she wouldn't be so particular, she told her; she'd take what she got. This made Margery mad and she hid the list, which she knew April and her mother loved looking at every night after supper. But April and her mother knew where it was—in the shoebox at the bottom of the closet—and they were familiar with every item on it. They had a game trying to guess which one Margery was working on: was she getting ready to take her shoes down to Little's to be dyed, or on her way to the hairdresser to look through the book of hairdos? Or going downtown to see if she could find a white piqué evening bag for under five dollars, or one of a dozen other things that had to be done before Friday night? When she was out, April and her mother would sneak into her room to see how much of the stuff she had piled up. Most of it was hidden, but between them they found the long gloves she had borrowed from Sally Croft, the silvery nylons she had bought, the pink compact her grandmother had given her as a kid and a half-empty pack of cigarettes, which came as a surprise only to April—her mother had seen Margery pulling one out when Eddie picked her up to go the movies. "She thinks she's so smart," was all she said, looking into the pack and counting how many were left. A minute later she was laughing at how neat everything was, everything just so. "Such a little lady she is, not a bit like you." The mother opened Margery's underwear drawer to look at the small stacks of underpants, the garter belt, the two bras, the dress shields. April was amazed Margery still didn't wear a girdle to hold up her stockings. "She doesn't need one." April knew it was coming. "I never asked *you* to wear one. You were the one who wanted one so bad. You're always in such a hurry."

"I need one, I'm fat."

"You're always knocking yourself, April. You don't need to do that, people will always do it for you." She was going to say more when they heard something downstairs. But it was only the little boy next door who had wandered over and was taking clothespins out of the milk box where April's mother kept them hidden.

Margery said she wasn't going to let them talk her into dropping in at the McLaughlins before the prom, but they said she looked so nice, and she *did* look nice, she admitted it, that she gave in. Eddie, who looked very stiff and shiny in his white jacket with his hair a little wet, had bought a yellow and white orchid in a wrist corsage and April thought Margery was going to have a fit. He said the florist had never heard of a colonial bouquet, they probably didn't make them anymore. Margery said they did too, but her mother had the clear plastic package open by then and she and April were oohing and ahing and making such a racket that Margery and the boy turned around to give them a look. How can you complain about getting an orchid? her mother said in a low voice, tying the satin ribbon around Margery's wrist. April thought the flower matched the dress exactly, but the boy wasn't paying attention to her thoughts. Someone had gotten the camera out and Margery and the boyfriend were being lined up against the living room wall just to the left of the wood fixture holding two Hummel figures and some glass knickknacks the grandmother had won at bingo. April could see Margery hadn't gotten over the flowers because she didn't want to stick her arm with

104

the orchid through Eddie's until her mother made her do it, and she was so rough one of the petals fell off.

April saw her mother follow Margery into the front hall closet to get the shawl she had borrowed from the lady next door. "You owe the woman the courtesy," April could hear her saying from the kitchen, "of showing her your dress and the nice flowers he got you, I don't care what you think of them." Margery said something, but April couldn't hear it. They were getting ready to leave. April's mother said to leave by the front door. April watched them through the living room window, her mother stood on the porch. "What's that, a Chevy?" her father said all of a sudden, and there he was at the other window. April said she didn't know, but guessed it was the mother's. She heard her father go back to the den and turn the TV on. Margery was in the car now and she even turned around to wave. April waved from the window and her mother waved from the porch, but Margery had already turned back and they drove off.

———

When they were on the avenue, Margery thought she might be feeling excited. Her mother had said to go ahead and enjoy herself while she had the chance and not waste it, so what if it isn't perfect, nothing's perfect. Margery looked over at Eddie driving, but she couldn't think of anything to say. "Are these your mother's car seats?"

"I borrowed them from my uncle."

They went past the drugstore, the newspaper stand, the furniture store, the Five and Ten, all closed for the night except the drugstore. They went by the beauty shop where Margery had gotten her hair done, a bun of curls on top of her head. "It's so stiff-feeling, Margery. Don't let him touch it," her mother said. She was glad it was stiff; that way it wouldn't come down no matter what. They turned down Harold Street and Margery rolled down the elbow-length gloves and took them off. "Those are nice, I like them," Eddie said, taking the key out of the ignition. Margery didn't want to touch anything with the gloves and spoil them and they wouldn't fit in the little purse, so when he offered to put them in his pocket, she gave them up and he stuffed them in there, the fingers sticking out of the flap.

When they got out of the car and Margery smoothed the puffy yellow skirt and patted the hard curls, she realized the effect wasn't right without the gloves—she could see it in the car window—so she took them back. "Don't let me touch anything."

Mrs. McLaughlin, seeing them from the upstairs parlor window, had come down to the first floor. "Don't. you. look. nice." she said, separating all the words. Right behind her were the people from downstairs, a retired couple. Across the street Margery had seen people looking out the window. She took Eddie's arm when he started up the steps ahead of her. The landing was dusty and she held the skirt up as high as she could, but there was already a scuff mark on the yellow shoe.

The people downstairs wanted them to step in a minute so they could get a picture, and they had to because Mrs. McLaughlin was pushing them in the door. The lady went into the kitchen and came back with a candy dish. Margery told her she couldn't pick one of the chocolates up in her glove. Mrs. McLaughlin suggested she put one in her purse to eat later, but the man had his Brownie camera out by then and lined the two of them up with the mother. "Come on, you're in this picture, too," he said, "you're part of it." The room was hot and Margery could hardly see because the shades were pulled and only one lamp on. There was a little square of light from the TV in the den. When the picture was taken, the lady asked them if they wouldn't sit a minute, but Margery said no, they were late, in an irritated voice, because she could smell a boiled dinner cooking and was sure her hair was going to smell like cabbage the rest of the night. Mrs. McLaughlin heard the tone and hustled them right upstairs before they tried to get away.

———

—What time'd you get home?

—Quarter of four, I heard her. I heard you. What time did you say you'd be home?

—I told you the post-prom didn't end till three. If I'd got home any earlier, I'd have been in an accident.

—Don't talk to your father in that tone. Did you have a good time?

—I guess.

—Did *he* have a good time?

—Yeah.

—Well, don't tell us anything about it, Margery. I only shelled out the twenty bucks so you could buy the new gown, but don't put yourself out for us.

—It was fun. . . . We danced—

—Did they sell Cokes in the basement like they do for the canteens?

—Don't interrupt. How did it look?

—They decorated it.

—Did you see people you know?

—Yeah, everybody looked nice.

—How was the feed? You know (Margery's father), Margery, that guy paid fifty dollars for those tickets. It had better be good, it didn't come cheap.

—It was nice. The Quonset Club. We had roast beef—

—Did you eat with your gloves on?

—No I didn't eat with my gloves on.

—What else did you do?

—We danced when we finished eating. It was a different band.

—Who?

—None of your business.

—What'd you do then?

—Well, some of them wanted to go down the beach.

—I told you I wanted you right home, God knows it was late enough as it is.

—I *came* right home. You're not listening to me. Some of them were going out for breakfast at the Shamrock Inn.

—Well, let their parents worry about them. Are you tired? you look tired.

—Mmm.

—What about his mother? Did you go see his mother like I told you?

—Yes.

—Did she like your dress?

—The people downstairs took a picture.

—Didn't his mother want a picture?

—I don't know. Maybe she doesn't have a camera.

—She doesn't have a camera!

—April, please, I'm trying to get it out of her and you keep butting in. Eat your breakfast, Margery, and go easy till you make up your rest. I don't want you getting sick on me now.

—I made up my rest already, I'm not tired.

—Just do what you're told, and don't forget to return all those things you borrowed. Don't make those people wait forever.

—Ma!

———

April was just going to the bathroom a minute, she told them, but on the way back she saw Margery spraying Windex ("What are you doing that for?") on her yellow shoes. There were paper-towel balls all over the floor, but the rest of the room was neat; the bed didn't look slept in. Margery didn't answer, but she didn't throw April out either. "Sit down. Not on the bed—can't you see I just made it? Sit on the floor and close the door." April sat and picked up one of the paper-towel balls. "Don't touch *anything*."

There was a knock on the door and their mother. She sat down on the bed without waiting for the invitation she knew wasn't coming. Margery sighed. She said she didn't feel like gabbing, she was too tired.

—You were going to tell her; you can tell me, too.

—I wasn't going to tell her. Who says I was going to tell her?

—She wasn't going to tell me, I was just sitting here.

Their mother got up. "I'll never forget this, Margery. You mark my words. You and your selfish sister can sit here all day for all I care. And after all I've done for you. I hope you have a real good time."

———

Margery and April could hear talk downstairs, then they heard someone on the stairs and the bedroom door close. April opened Margery's door a crack, but now that was *him* on the stairs (April jumped back and tried to get behind Margery, but Margery was already up and pushed April toward the door).

"Thanks," yanks the door open, face all red, "thanks a lot for doing this to your mother." April could see his hands shaking. If he was going to hit, he would have done it by now, but he didn't; he just stood there and looked like he was going to, then went out, slamming the door so hard the windows shook. They could hear him on the stairs. April was going to tell Margery that she had a box of Crackerjacks under the bed if they got hungry later, but before she even got it out, Margery told her she was a jerk and to get out. April was surprised to see how immature Margery was getting again.

Providence, 1960:
Cavities

The Italian peddlers were out with their fruit and vegetable carts, backed up as far as the dentists' office, my mother's old dentist: Alfred, Louis, Stanley, and Ira Meiklejohn. We thought about them up there, having their fingers bit. But we passed on to Amore's window, full of First Communion dresses, with the prices written on index cards.

My mother picked a nice summer squash; she had her fingers around one, pimply and 12¢ a pound. When the I (my mother called them "I's") put the squash in the bag, my mother picked off a seedless grape and ate it.

The bakery shop was next. The bell over the door rang, and the old lady hustled right out to see if we were stealing. I looked at the things I liked: cruller with cracked glaze, stale vanilla frosting on a spice bar, tapioca in the cherry pie, yellow pudding in the hole of the puff pastry; on the counter was a waxed paper and twelve greasy squares where the pizza slices had been. My mother laced her arm around her pocketbook strap and leaned against the pole in the middle of the shop. She always looked weary when she had to spend money. A cocoanut cream pie—the closest she could come to a vegetable—is what she picked out. She also bought me a hermit. When I walked outside, I almost tripped on a TV antenna someone had dropped on the sidewalk. Hurry up, she said.

The I's weren't doing that good, she said, probably because the weather wasn't too hot. I watched them while we waited for the light; some of them were filling in the empty spots in their mounds of fruit, rolling the apples and tomatoes to make sure they were showing their good side. Some of them were so short, they had to stand on stools to reach, but they could count the nickles and dimes, my mother said. The sky started to get dark and we jumped from umbrella to umbrella, then made a run for it to Amore's doorway.

The First Communion dresses were on hangers hooked onto clotheslines that were strung back and forth across the window. The skirts were stuffed with tissue paper to make them stick out. My mother pointed out the dress with the pleated skirt, which wasn't supposed to stick out, but which was stuffed with paper anyway, and buckled all around the middle; she laughed. There was a skithery looking cotton dress which she said would lay flat no matter what you did to it. The day after my First Communion, she kept talking about how it all looked, the straggly line to the altar, every girl with a different dress on, some sticking straight out like ballet skirts, some flat as a door; some yellow, some white; the I's with their pearl chokers and rhinestones, the Irish girls with limp satin in the old styles; the two girls whose fathers were doctors, in white cotton with pleated skirts and a string of pearls. The tall girls with blotchy knees; the fat girls with thick legs; the girls who had developed early and had hairy legs. The rain was letting up, and we stuck our heads out of the doorway. But it started right up again, and we ran back.

Some of the dresses were pinned to pink paper lying on the floor, and some were clothespinned to the wire that the window drape was hung on, but my mother wasn't looking anymore. She was watching the street. An old man in a fedora with the brim all turned down was trying to close the umbrella over his fruit wagon. It was stuck. The ends were flapping in the wind; the rain was coming in under the sides; all the vegetables were getting wet, and the green paper under them. He wiped his hands on his apron and tried again; then he took the umbrella off, still open. We could see the water rolling off the sides of the wagon, making big wet marks on the wood. He had the umbrella on the sidewalk with his foot up in the spines trying to kick the lock open. My mother hoped he wasn't having a heart attack. Another fruit man with a newspaper on his head ran over yelling instructions: jiggle it, he said, but the old man probably couldn't understand English. The umbrella rolled into the gutter while the old man tried to lay planks over his cart; he let it stay there, wide open. It started rolling into the middle of the street and he ran after it; the cars honked, and another Italian ran into the street and stopped the cars until the old man had caught up with it and dragged it over to the sidewalk again; it closed right away. My mother noticed he hadn't sold very much. His heap of tomatoes and beans was very smooth, but I saw that a box of strawberries was gone. The cars whizzed by; we had been standing in that doorway a long time.

It seemed to be letting up and after three more red lights we walked down the street toward the bus stop. We passed the dentists' office again and looked up at the cardboard signs in the second-story windows: each cardboard was printed with the name of a different Meicklejohn. My mother was not from Providence, but as soon as she had moved here—when I was a baby—the lady downstairs told her about the Meiklejohn dentists on Federal Hill and she went there to have a cavity filled. The lady downstairs said they were cheap and you didn't need an appointment. My mother took the bus and got off at Broad and Federal. First thing she did was read off the names of all the brothers, printed over the doorbell. She didn't know which one to go to, but thought it was funny how they all had become dentists, all from the same family. The staircase was funny too; it was wide and there were rubber treads on either side. The Meiklejohns shared a floor with an eye doctor, and she wondered if they didn't expect the one set of patients to use one side and the other set, the other side. She went up on the right-hand side. Once she had dropped the Meiklejohns as our dentist, we started going to the eye doctor. She told us just for the fun of it to pretend we were really going to the dentist; then only at the last minute, on the threshhold of the Meiklejohn waiting room, did we spin around and run down the corridor to the door with the eyeglasses printed on it.

It was a hot day, that first time, and even the sidewalk smelled of chemicals; the smell got worse the higher you climbed. No one was with her. The reception room was filled with old people, mostly Italians in black coats. All the magazines were old with ripped covers; the shade was open and the sun was blazing in, blinding everybody, but the nurse said she couldn't close it. Dust was on everything. There was an orange flower arrangement attached to the wall. Everybody was speaking Italian.

Through the window you could see all the street vendors and people walking in between the carts. There were some men standing in front of the bakery; they didn't move a muscle the whole time she was in there. She had to wait an hour just to get into the dentist's office. When they finally called her in (it was a Meiklejohn; they all wore glasses), a nurse put a barber towel around her neck. Then they left her there to wait. There was a window with a green Venetian blind and she watched the fruit vendors (who were only doing so-so that day). She could hear breathing, and people dropping things into the sterilizer. They lead a hard life, those fruit men, she told me; that old man, she said, would probably much rather be sitting out on his porch or in his backyard instead of selling fruit and vegetables in the heat with a heavy sweater on. The dentist's office wasn't air conditioned, but she said it was freezing all the same. They made her wait another half hour, then one of the Meiklejohns came in and looked at her mouth. He had gray hair and a line right through the middle of his glasses. Then he went out the door and she had to wait another fifteen minutes. A different Meiklejohn came in with trifocals on, and used the drill. About ten minutes later, the same Meiklejohn came back with the cement and a pick and a mirror. Spit, he said. "He kept telling me to spit," my mother said, "but I couldn't spit with his finger in my mouth." The sterilizer started wheezing and this Meiklejohn threw all his metal tools in there. She could smell something burning then. A rubber glove was sticking to the handle, the thumb was melting down the side of the case. Another Meiklejohn came in and smoothed down the filling with a pick. The nurse scraped the glove off the sterilizer with a putty knife. The dentist handed my mother a paper cup in a silver cup and told her to drink and spit. He didn't say one other word to me, my mother said, the whole time. My mother spat out a whole mouthful of silver splinters. She could see them in the bottom of the sink. Then the dentist walked out and another wandered in. He picked around in there for a while, she said; she could hear another drill going, running water, the sterilizer steaming. You could still smell burning rubber. Finally, she jumped down off the seat. They didn't even wind it down. The receptionist unclipped the towel off her neck. My mother paid the money. "I walked down the other side of the staircase," she said, "the eye doctor's." She always had us do that too; you always knew you were free of the dentist when you were safe on the eye doctor's side.

I could see my ankles reflected in the black glass at the bottom of the dentist's building. I stooped to pull up my socks. The elastics holding them up had moved and were stuck to the hair on my legs. There was no one going in or out of the dentists' office, so she opened the door to let me take a sniff.

The umbrellas were all up again. The old man had decided to move himself to a better spot, but he had pushed his cart right in front of the driveway to the bank parking lot and the cops told him to move along. Now he couldn't get his umbrella to go up, so he just lay it across his cart and started pushing. My mother said it must be rusted. She reached into her pocketbook for a quarter. We followed the vendor down the street; he was going in our direction, toward the bus stop. My mother told me to walk slow. It was noontime and the sun was heating up the street, causing steam to come up out of the gutters. All of a sudden, the old man turned down a sidestreet and we lost him.

One of Them
Gets Married

April was eighteen and a half and away at school, St. Bernard's College in Wrentham, all girls, when Margery married an Italian and would have given her father a heart attack, on top of everything else, if things hadn't changed since the old days, but they had. Mrs. Dooley died of cancer in 1969. They had her up at the institution for a year, thought she had gone mental, then someone discovered the tumor and gave her five months to live but she died in one. Sad funeral, her father told April when she came home Thanksgiving; a lovely woman, he said, and all those kids. The kids were married except for Terrence, who had gone into the seminary early, come out, gone in again when he was seventeen, and was now buying and selling property, as her father put it; condemned buildings, was what her mother said. Married, little Alice Dooley already had three of her own. Her father said this at least six times. Alice and her husband moved out-of-state, he told her another time; she was pregnant with the fourth and they were hoping for a boy, three girls and a boy, but her real interest in life (April knew by this kind of talk that her father was drinking again) was to get as fat as she could and now she was already big as a house. April had never heard him so cynical. He had white hair now; he had made himself go white, Margery said, because he was anxious to be dead and get it over with. Their mother—she was not white, but had her hair done at the Palace Beauty Salon; autumn auburn was the color she used until it got brassy and they mixed it with medium light brown—told Margery she shouldn't talk like that. Oh nobody around here should do anything but you,

115

Margery said in that tone no one liked. What did she say? their mother asked April. Don't tell me; two of the world's biggest hypocrites you are. Well here (handing the dishtowel to April), if you're so smart, you can take over my job and see if you can keep this stinking family going. She was going to leave the room in a temper but Margery left instead: I've had it, she said, I'm getting out of here.

"Tell me (to April), you're smart, what's gotten into her?" Before April could say anything—and she had her ideas; she had been taking psychology for a year now just so she could tackle problems like this and was only too willing—her mother said, "Oh I know, it's getting married. If she's upset now, just think how she'll be after, if she thinks this is bad." April sat down, but her mother had gotten up already and was at the foot of the stairs yelling to Margery to bring down the magazines and show her sister here the patterns she had picked for her china and silver.

"I don't feel like it."

"Well, just throw them down. I'll show her if you won't."

"I'll show her. I don't want you showing her."

They looked at the pictures and Margery told stories about the big Italian dinners she had gone to at the Tagliatellas, with all the relatives and a hundred and one courses, one right on top of the other. You'll get money from them, her mother said; they like to give money for weddings, but I'll tell them your patterns anyway, they can afford a couple of place settings at least.

"Ma!"

"What do you mean 'Ma?' You'll be glad to have it. They don't bring home much from Unemployment you know (Joey Tag, as Margery called him, worked for the state), get it while you can."

They were starting up again. April said she had studying to do.

"Don't clutter. I just broke my back cleaning."

Other things had changed. They didn't say the Mass in Latin, the nuns wore dresses and you could see their hair. The old ones looked older in street clothes, April thought, but the poor things are cooler in summer—that's what everybody said. The pastor had died; April was away at school for the funeral, but her father said he had brass from the state house and the chancellery: the bishop, the auxiliary

116

bishop, and a bishop nobody knew from out-of-state. They put on the dog, April's father said, but then, this is a big parish to open up all of a sudden, a real plum for whoever gets it. Your friend's uncle there, you know, Fr. O'Reilly, that cousin of the Dooleys, they say he's high on the list. I'd like to see a man like that get it, do the parish good.

They had bingo at the church Saturday nights after cutting out Saturday confessions. But the real blow came, her father told April, when the acting pastor announced in the church bulletin that he was forced to hire a lay person to teach at Holy Savior. There just weren't enough vocations to go around; people aren't making the sacrifice, April's father said. It's a scandal when a parish this size can't produce the vocations to staff the parochial school. Thank God my kids aren't there anymore.

April wondered if he were criticizing her for not making the sacrifice, but he had hardly noticed when she went up to St. Bernard's in the fall instead of off to the Mother House to be a postulant, after she had announced her vocation the year she started high, and every year after. Her mother noticed. "See, I told you you'd outgrow it." But even *she* didn't rub it in. April couldn't imagine ever wanting to be a nun. One of the first things the lay theology teacher had given her when she explained she was doing a year of college before maybe joining a semi-cloistered order in Providence was a book about the crimes the pope had committed in World War II. She brought home another book by a minister about God's death and by then, starting to have different thoughts and wondering whether to bother going to Mass or not; it didn't seem to matter. There was only the one discussion at home about this change, when her mother asked her if she thought she was smarter than God. It struck April as funny, but she didn't laugh out loud.

"The church doesn't have the support it used to," her father was saying. They were sitting together on the porch. "My mother and father built that church with their collection money; they wouldn't be able to build a shack with the pittance they get Sundays. You're lucky if some of them show up for Palm Sunday and Christmas, doing you a big favor to be there, too."

He was talking about the Italians. The parish had always had Italians, but now they were moving into the neighborhood and taking over. Two Irish families had moved out just this year down the street, he said (April couldn't think whom he meant until she remembered the two old ladies in the Gallagher house, and the old guy, Mr. Burke, dead now, who rented a room over Adams Drugstore and had to be put in the institution), and Italians moved in. Young children too, he said, so they'll be around for a while. You can hear the mothers shrieking, he said, up and down the street all hours of the night. You can always hear mothers, April wanted to say, Italian or not. She was too flip these days, they were always saying, especially for a college girl.

Other things had changed. The mayor had left his wife for a hair-dresser, and the name dragged in the mud, April's father said. He wasn't reelected to the fifth term. Who'd they elect? A Guinea, he said, Carbone, first time in the city's history. Not only was it an Italian, but Republican party. "Oh, they're thrilled up there on the Hill, first place urban renewal goes, you watch; they're tickled pink."

Margery's Guinea (her father called him that only to April) had at least gone to junior college and was trying to make something of himself, which was more than he could say for most of them. Joey Tag had made himself into an insurance man before his uncle got him in at Unemployment. He had worked for Metropolitan Life down the avenue across from the drugstore, and Margery and her mother used to go down and peek in the window. "He looks busy in there," her mother said, "you can at least say that for him."

April was not surprised to hear that Margery and her mother were doing things together. Margery had changed, or maybe the mother had changed, but they were thick now, that's how her father put it, and went everywhere together.

Her mother had gotten Margery a job at the butterfly valve company she worked for. Margery was a clerk typist across the hall in accounts receivable. They loved to talk about the "personalities" at work. The mother was always coming home with a tale about how the younger guys were trying their best to get in with her so she'd put in a good word with Margery. Her mother loved the attention, April could see that.

"And such a stick in the mud she is. I tell her to have her fun now *before* she's married and cooped up. But she won't give them the right

118

time of day, so stuck she is on that Joey. I can tell you're really in love, Margery." April didn't know whether she was kidding or not.

The wedding was a week from Saturday. They were going to be married by Fr. Doyle, April's friend from high school, used to run the CYO and take them to skating parties till he decided all of a sudden to go down to the missions in Peru. There was nothing left for him to do in Providence, was what he told April and she never forgot the weird look on his face when he said it (probably losing his marbles, her mother said at the time). Fr. Doyle hoped they—the kids in the CYO, April figured, although it was just herself there during one of the vocation sessions they had twice a week—would help him make the sacrifice.

He went away in February after they announced it over the pulpit at all the Masses. April's mother said she felt sad, because he was a holy man and not like the other phonies with a new Buick every year. He came back the next summer. April's father heard he'd had a nervous collapse and the bishop shipped him to Narragansett to recuperate. At first, they weren't going to let him back in at Holy Savior, even though he wanted to come back. Eventually, he did get back. "He was good with the kids," April's mother piped up from the kitchen. That's what they say, her father said, but you and I know it had a lot to do with that cousin of his that's a bishop of Hartford or something. Anyway, he got back in (April's father), and you were embarrassed running into him on the street, you didn't know what to say. "He looked like Hell," the mother said, "skin and bones, lost all his hair." Next thing you know, April's father went on, they're rushing him to Rhode Island Hospital dying of cancer, although I heard from someone they had him drying out up there. If you were still in good with him (to April), you could get the real story.

But it was Margery who was friends with Fr. Doyle now. She got to know him (April's mother) in that ecumenical group she was involved with when she was dating the funny guy from Cumberland, remember him? But I could have told her she'd never marry that guy—plus, he had diabetes to boot. Once a week, she and that Charlie Muncie, I think his name was, went up to the rectory with one other couple and two single girls who left the convent and wanted a little exposure to life, that's what Margery said, but they picked a funny place to get it.

Margery kept going to the sessions even after Charlie was gone, and no more danger of a mixed marriage. The group dwindled to just the two girls; the nuns had departed too. "We talk," April heard Margery telling her mother; "sometimes we go out for coffee." Is he okay? the mother wanted to know. "You wouldn't recognize him, he's so different-acting. Always criticizing you-know-who." April thought for a minute this might be herself, but it had to mean the new pastor nobody liked.

Does he ever say to say hi to me? (April from the dining room).

I wasn't talking to you so just butt out.

I'd just like to know, Margery.

No.

He must say *something*.

April had run into Fr. Doyle once on the avenue. He spoke, but she could tell he didn't know who it was. Maybe it's because I've lost so much weight, she told her mother. Oh, I think he recognized you, April, her mother said; he just didn't want to admit it. You know how they are when they've been on sick leave, they don't like people judging them.

"I'm not judging him." (An old friend of April's who knew Fr. Doyle in the old days and was the only girl from St. Mary's Academy to go up to Brown University, non-Catholic, said she wasn't surprised he didn't recognize her; he was probably in bad faith. April explained that meant a bad conscience. She always goes too far, was what her mother said to this.)

———————

Margery got married at the ten o'clock Mass, riding down with her girlfriend Harriet and April in a limousine from the Callaghan Funeral Home. "This is how he does business," her father told April about Buddy Callaghan, the funeral director. "I told him he already had this family, he didn't have to worry, but he always extends the courtesy. All he asks is to get invited to the wedding so people can see him there."

Nothing seemed funny about the limousine, Margery told April when she asked, it was just a limousine. "Don't *you* get started," her

120

mother said from the bathroom. That was Thursday, two days before the wedding when things were at their worst.

————

"The bride wore an off-white sateen gown with Venice lace and empire waist," they read on Sunday, sitting at the kitchen table eating from a foil-covered platter of cold roast beef and ham. The picture had come out too dark and on the second to the last page with weddings from out of town. Margery was next to a Polish girl—Irene Dombrowski to Harold Zinciewicz—which didn't help matters. She was still a pretty girl, her father kept saying over and over. No one paid any attention; April saw her mother rolling her eyes. "I'm sick of weddings; I don't want to go to another wedding for the next ten years," she said. April could tell she was pleased.

She had never had so much fun in her life, April had heard her mother say at the wedding. She had been up dancing the whole night. She had danced with the neighbors, with April's Uncle Bernie, with the bridegroom's father. She had danced more than Margery had. She was up and down all afternoon too, having to talk to people and introduce them to the bridegroom's family. They kept coming over—his mother and father—and telling the bride to bring their son over to the table, somebody wanted to talk to him. "Already," Margery said to April, "they're making me out to be his servant." "Are you talking to me?" April said. Margery got up, took the bridegroom by the arm and led him over to the table of relatives.

Margery had not spoken to April before the wedding. She was grouchy all the time and could not even take the trouble (her mother) to be civil to the people who were forking over the money so she could have the goddamned wedding in the first place. April could see she wasn't having the kind of fun you read about in the bride magazines. She acted as it if were an ordeal, even getting the presents. The only thing she got excited about was when his mother sent over two antique gold candlesticks which had been the grandmother's in the old country. Margery said she never expected anything that good. Her mother was making a joke to April about how hideous they were and Margery would have to drag them out every time she had the in-laws, as she called them, over to dinner. Margery said they could both go to hell. April thought the two of them would have another blow-out, but her mother acted as if she hadn't heard it. Later April heard her mother telling their father's Aunt Helen, "as high hat (April's grandmother) as they come," that Margery had gotten a set of solid gold candlesticks from his people. Aunt Helen said they'd be expecting something in return for that. April's mother overlooked that comment. "The girl's thrilled," she said, "you'd think it was a million dollars."

"I should say so," said Aunt Helen, all red in the face from the hot roast beef and two glasses of cold duck. Each table had a carafe of wine—that was part of the package deal they had from the caterers. After that, it was paying for your own. "That's the best your father and I can do for you, Margery," her mother said, "so don't knock it. She'll be wanting a wedding too sooner or later and your father's got to give one what he gives the other; fair's fair."

———

Margery and Joey rented a tenement over in the Fruit Hill neighborhood. Margery and her mother spent the month before the wedding fixing it up. They scrubbed the bathroom tile with toothbrushes, laid in shelfpaper, and washed and waxed all the floors. It was backbreaking work, April's mother wrote in a letter to her, describing all the jobs they had done in detail, "and that Margery's no ball of fire either. She let me do most of it."

When April came home for the weekend, her father took her right over to the tenement. ("You take her," the mother said, "I'm sick of the place.") He told April what they were paying, that it was an ideal location—so handy to the bus lines—and how nice the girl had fixed it up. He was the most excited about it. April had never seen him so excited. He ran up the flight of stairs and pulled April in the door. She saw the whole place: the linen closet, the back hall, the kitchen cabinets with the everyday glasses they had gotten at the January sale at Sears, the broom closet. The new dinette set and the bedroom set were there but otherwise the place was empty, except for the braided rug (my aunt, he said) in the living room. "You'd like something like this, wouldn't you?" April said she would. "You'll have your turn, just wait and see. You're both beautiful girls. Don't belittle yourself," he said, when he saw the smile. "You'll do as good as her easy, plus you've got the education. Don't be in a hurry," he said. "Be smart. You can get married any time."

The way he said this, so friendly and enthusiastic, made April feel enthusiastic. They were both enthusiastic and looked through all the rooms again, but in the car there was nothing to say all the way home.

"What did you say to him (April's mother) that got him into such a stinking mood?"

He was on and off like that right up till the day of the wedding: full of it (April's mother) one minute; sitting in the dark smoking a cigarette, the next. When he got like that, everybody tiptoed around and made sure not to slam the cupboard doors and best just to stay out of his way. April was starting abnormal psych at school and paid close attention to the symptoms of all the mental diseases, but she couldn't find one that fit him and his ways. Margery and her mother didn't think there was anything wrong with him. "He (the mother) brings it on himself, *we* know that much." But April didn't think the things he was doing were normal. He was still up during the night throwing up, but they were used to that. It was more the things he did during the day. Sometimes at dinner he just stared at the wall and sighed. He looked unhappy—that was one way to describe it, April thought— but there was more. "You have to remember to handle him with kid gloves," April's mother kept saying, "and that's something *you* can't seem to learn how to do."

Sometimes April thought she was better off at school, but she wasn't happy there either. Margery told her she was lucky to be away and should thank her lucky stars, rotten roommate or not. When April told her mother how the girls in her end of the hall were against her, her mother said she should learn not to let people walk all over her. "You were always like that, you know, a doormat."

Seeing Margery's tenement and thinking about what it would be like to live there—Joey Tag, easy-going and cute—even though it was small and everything old-fashioned, funny colors, gave April the idea that even for her, things might get better by and by, as her grandmother said. She could always get married and move out of the dorm junior year. She told Margery how lucky she was. Margery shrugged, but April knew she'd been dying to get married.

"You can get married too, anybody can. It doesn't take talent— *they* did."

Who?

"Them. Them, stupid," pointing downstairs, "who do you think I meant, Jackie Kennedy? Don't kid yourself, April, nobody's got it that great. You're so naïve. Who's that happy you know? If you'd get your nose out of a book once in a while, you'd see the world and see how it stinks."

April didn't think she'd ever heard Margery talk like this before. Even though it was negative, it was something Margery was telling her personally and she was grateful. When Margery saw this—and she never (her mother) missed a trick—she told April to get out, she was going to take a nap.

Providence, 1966: Ducks and Lucks

Msgr. Rigney had already been made a monsignor when he came ten years ago to the Church of the Holy Savior. With him he brought a pair of red dachshunds and a black station wagon. The housekeeper knew what that meant: each of the curates could have his own car plus, if the monsignor would agree to borrow one of their sedans once in a while, the nuns could use the station wagon. A perfect car for a big man, she had thought, seeing him for the first time, using both hands to hoist himself out of the front seat.

And next week he was going to be sixty-six. She watched him on that little square of lawn between the convent and the rectory. She could see the short black boots he liked to wear sticking out from under his long cassock. The dogs were tangled up in their leashes, but he was reading his breviary and wasn't paying them any attention. When he walked up near the sacristy entrance of the church, they both lifted a leg, and the monsignor had to pull them away quickly or risk committing a sacrilege, she expected. People didn't necessarily think he was less saintly because of being so fat, but they did like to comment about it. You could see him panting as he climbed up the altar steps. Sometimes he was so out of breath, he just stood there a minute in front of the tabernacle, and everybody held their breath down the center aisle for fear he would have a heart attack. Now people were worried he might have the gout. His shoes hurt so much he walked on the edges of his feet. He had thin hair and they could see the fold of fat on the back of his neck; his chasuble cracked loudly every time he bent to kiss the altar stone. From the side you could see that he couldn't quite reach, but not everybody knew that.

He had been the first to bring pets to the rectory and it had taken some getting used to, she told people. But they never had an accident, knock on wood, or barked in the middle of the night. They were good dogs for such temperamental types. (No one she knew owned a dachshund.) They ate only regular dog food, she told anyone who asked, and their names were Dox and Lux. Ducks and Lucks, she had thought initially until the pastor had taken a piece of paper to write both words out. Now every time Mrs. Whelan mentioned the dogs, she spelled their names, unless people knew them very well.

He liked his breakfast at 8:45, immediately after the eight o'clock Mass, but he always waited for the curate (usually it was Father Doyle, the youngest) to de-vest and get himself comfortable. He didn't eat lunch at all, she told people, and this always made the women parishioners more apt to take his side when their husbands made light of him. He liked dinner served at 6:30, quarter to seven, and Mrs. Whelan always had it ready a few minutes early in case he couldn't wait. First she fed the dogs; then they crawled under the table and lay on his feet. The assistant pastor (Fr. Flynn, older than Fr. Doyle, but much younger than the pastor) tried throwing them table scraps, but the monsignor wouldn't hear of it. He feels people will talk, Mrs. Whelan conjectured. She should hope so, the lady she was chatting with said, considering what some people in the neighborhood have to eat.

Mrs. Whelan was surprised to learn from her tone that there was—between the pastor and the bulk of his parishioners—not only the matter of his weight, and the fact of his not being born in the parish, but also the dogs. People didn't like it that he had brought dogs. He only feeds them that cheap, dry food, she said, and out of his own pocket. She still wondered if the lady had gotten the story straight. Not long after, it came back to the rectory that the monsignor was feeding his dogs at the table.

He's awfully good with the sick, she told people. Saturday afternoons, when a lot of them would be up at the track, he spends an hour or two at the veterans' hospital. The head nurse had told her, she said, that he was very human with them, that he was a great favorite. And he was always bringing things home with him—not that he wants anything, but he doesn't want to hurt their feelings. She would like to have had a key to his room so she could show the cufflinks, the rosary from the Pacific, the travelogue, the book of poems; there were also perishables, which she couldn't very well show. He doesn't eat any of it himself, she said; sometimes he'll give it over to the convent, or to us. What she would like to have said, and was going to say one of these days, was that he didn't eat that much rich food. I would know it if he did, she wanted to say; after all, I see everything they eat. He eats exactly what they eat. Some people—she did mention to one of the nuns—are fat because of nature. The nun suggested it would be best not to discuss the fathers among themselves. One of the ladies who worked part-time at the rectory asked why she was always sticking up for him; nobody was criticizing, she said. But Mrs. Whelan had grown up in Holy Savior's and she knew what people criticized and what they wouldn't. She had been worried since the day he arrived and couldn't get out of his station wagon.

His mother, God rest her soul, the one who converted, said he had always been fat. The mother, before she died, came around every Thursday afternoon. The custodian would help carry her wheelchair up the rectory steps and the pastor would wheel her down to his own parlor. Mrs. Rigney liked to talk too, and had told Mrs. Whelan about the time the monsignor had had to go to confession three times in one week for laughing at Sexagesima Sunday, He's like that, you know, she said, can get real silly over nothing. Mrs. Whelan didn't understand. I don't know why it struck us so funny, the convert said, but it did. We laughed so hard—I didn't know, she added, that he would have to confess. Both ladies were silent. Mrs. Whelan didn't understand what was so funny, but she was glad the monsignor had the sense to get to confession. The other housekeeper thought the story was stupid. The nun who emptied the budget envelopes every Sunday said it might have been sacriligious. One of the parishioners, the wife of the president of the Holy Name Society, said she always thought "that one" was a queer bird, but now she could see where he got it from.

Mrs. Whelan knew well that if the pastor hadn't come from another parish, it wouldn't have been half so bad, but the people were still mad that the bishop—who *had* been brought up in Holy Savior's—hadn't thought enough of them to assign one of their own. They think the bishop did them dirt, she told the housekeeper early on, before she got to know Msgr. Rigney. The bishop didn't make matters any better when he sent four painted portraits of himself to the pastor, who immediately had them installed in the school, in the convent, in the hallway of the rectory and in the back of the church, where they sell the leaflets and the candles. A lot of people took to calling him by his last name after that.

No one had any special gripe against the monsignor, except he was not the kind of man they expected.

———

Mrs. Whelan always waited till one of them came home before turning the lights on, lighting the long corridor length by length. The walls were light green and a little grimy in the light; the globes on the ceiling were dulled by dust, but the floor was spotless; it was washed and waxed every week. There were swirls left on the green linoleum from the buffer and his boot heels squeaked on the polish. His neck and feet ached from standing through the litany of the saints, which had concluded the Forty Hours devotion. The church was half full, he told Mrs. Whelan. He pushed his bedroom door open and felt the dogs' weight on the other side. The lights went on behind him and he could hear somebody pacing. He sat down and eased the boot off, rubbing his arches. One of the dogs sniffed the boot and knocked it over. He pulled them nearer by their collars, and lifted one onto his lap.

Someone had left the window open and the dampness cooled his neck; his hand stuck to the arm of the chair. It was a little after eight and the streetlight made a satin puddle on his linoleum, turning the dog's red back silvery. The smoke from his cigar rose up through the glare at the window. He didn't have any energy. Cars going down School Street lifted the air around him, but they stopped too after a while. It wasn't perfectly dark; you could still make out the ribs of the radiator, the wooden bars on the back of the straight chair, the laundry bag on the doorknob of the closet, the braided palm looped through the crosspiece of his ebony crucifix, ordination present from his own parish.

He had been sitting there half an hour when he turned on the lights. He moved to the desk and looked at the dark outline of the maple tree and his own egglike shadow. The dogs were too little to be reflected, but they were standing right by him. He sat down.

This Sunday's sermon would be based on the miracle of the loaves and fishes. He opened his missal, but there was no illustration. Mrs. Whelen had once told him she always thought of the loaves as snowflake rolls, with a slightly crisper crust. He told her the fish were like sardines (edible raw, he said), but not as small as sardines. If they had been as small as sardines, he said, how could so many people have filled themselves up on so few?

If the fish and loaves were grace, then it would be true to say grace is impossible without the intercession of God. Human strength is inadequate; there are only two resources available to man: faith and good works. Faith, he wrote, requires a childlike patience with the ways of God. The multitude had to be patient because Jesus had things to say to them, and their patience had to be tested before the miracle could occur. It is God, ultimately, who fills us, he wrote, like he filled the multitude with twelve loaves and two fishes. We must be empty and wait for God. We must not be frustrated; we must not despair of the prospect of salvation in the desert. At first God's grace is light, unnoticeable; it is pure air, purer than breath; it is the air of salvation, which is light and completely satisfying. It was coming very easily and he wrote another page and lay down his ballpoint.

The canopy over the pulpit, cast in the shape of a seashell, shed a large disc of yellow light which fell on him and the green marble floor below. The sharp light made his red hair look like a small hat; his glasses flashed under the spotlights; she could see two gold discs on the lenses from way at the back of the center aisle. You couldn't see the steps leading to the pulpit, so it looked as if he were coming out of the wall. He wore a white brocaded vestment with a lily on the front and back. You'd think his mouth would be dry, but his words passed through the microphone and into the well of the congregation clear and undistorted. He passed a loaf and fish to every open face.

He gave the charge of the rest of the loaves to the men in the back holding the collection baskets. Pass the fresh ones, he thought, just as soon as they finish with what they've got. He counted the rows. In his loosely constructed talk, he linked the loaves to the thin white hosts; in his own mind, he linked those thin white hosts to the raised dots on the tongues, to the dotted lights on the gold plate held under the chins. He lay a fish on each tongue. It was hot under the lights and his glasses slipped. Emptiness, he said, is a godlike quality. He could see that they weren't all empty yet, so he kept talking, even though it was already 9:30 on a Sunday morning, and the Nine was usually out by then.

He climbed back down the narrow white steps and crossed in front of the altar, his black heels barely making a sound on the marble tiles. He enunciated with clarity the prayers of the Offertory; he emphasized the bones of the Mass, the movements from left to right, the bows, the opening of the hands, the lifting of the cup: everything that was hard, minimal, with a hollow in the middle. He lay hosts on the tongues. He concentrated even harder. He filled the emptiness with his breath and they could hear his breathing all the way down the center aisle, where she heard it and thought he might be having a heart attack.

Jean McGarry has published fiction and prose poems in *Sulfur*, the *New Orleans Review, Antioch Review, Stand*, and other literary magazines. She teaches English at the University of Missouri–Columbia.

The Johns Hopkins University Press

Airs of Providence

This book was composed in Goudy Old Style text and display type by Brushwood Graphics Studio, from a design by Chris L. Smith. It was printed on 60-lb. Glatfelter paper and bound in Joanna Kennett by Thomson-Shore, Inc.